THE SECRETS OF

Blueberries,
Brothers,
MOOSE
& Me

THE SECRETS OF
Blueberries,
Brothers,
MOOSE
& Me

SARA NICKERSON

DUTTON CHILDREN'S BOOKS
AN IMPRINT OF PENGUIN GROUP (USA) LLC

DUTTON CHILDREN'S BOOKS
Published by the Penguin Group
Penguin Group (USA) LLC
375 Hudson Street
New York, New York 10014

USA | Canada | UK | Ireland | Australia
New Zealand | India | South Africa | China

penguin.com
A Penguin Random House Company

Library of Congress Cataloging-in-Publication Data
CIP Data is available.

ISBN 978-0-525-42654-7

Printed in the United States of America
1 3 5 7 9 10 8 6 4 2

Edited by Julie Strauss-Gabel
Book design by Irene Vandervoort

For my brothers—
Dan, Dave, Jay, and Jim—
who still stick together out there

THE SECRETS OF

Blueberries,
Brothers,
MOOSE
& Me

CHAPTER 1

MY OLDER BROTHER, PATRICK, CAME UP WITH THE idea. He was nearly fourteen and it was his summer of protein drinks and hundred-a-day push-ups to stop from being so skinny. Something had happened to him, something that made him hide out in the bathroom, examining his thin arms and legs in the full-length mirror. By the end of that summer, I'd know what it was. I'd also know about the blood feud between two farmers, and how it felt to have tiny chunks of gravel lodged in my face. But I'm getting ahead.

One thing I did know, right from the start, was that my brother was desperate for new clothes, and not the new-to-us thrift store variety we usually wore. So halfway through the summer, when he started searching for jobs that a fourteen-year-old could have, I knew he was thinking ahead to September, and the new school year, and jeans with actual store tags.

"Look, Mom!" he said. It was a socked-in rainy day, and we'd already spent most of it watching black-and-white Western movies on TV.

My mother, she loves old Westerns. I'm pretty sure it's because they are about as far from real life as a person can get. Ladies wear long skirts, horses scramble up rocky cliffs, and fat tumbleweeds bounce across wagon-track roads, making dust fly. Best of all, the good guy always wins and the bad guy gets locked up or chased out of town.

Mom sat on the couch with her legs tucked under her while Claude, my baby brother, napped on her lap. "Look, Mom," Patrick said again. He pointed to a small ad in one of those free newspapers, the kind you get outside grocery stores.

I slid off the couch, pulled the 3-D glasses from my shirt pocket, and settled close to my brother. When I leaned over his shoulder he didn't tell me to move and he didn't even snort at my glasses. Instead, he just pointed to where his finger had already made a small black smear in the middle of the page.

KIDS!!! EARN MONEY, HAVE FUN!
PICK BERRIES @MOOSE G'S BLUEBERRY FARM,
42 CENTS/POUND
BEST PICKER WINS PRIZE!!!

"Wow," I said. It was like we'd stumbled upon the biggest secret in the history of the world. Money! Money for picking!

In my mind I saw us standing in an orchard, grabbing bills off branches and stuffing them deep into the pockets of our brand-new jeans. "I could do that, too. Couldn't I, Patrick? Couldn't I?" I held my breath waiting.

My brother studied the advertisement again. His finger underlined each word. *Earn money. Have fun.* He said, "How many pounds do you think we could pick?" And just like that, we were a team.

I thought about a blueberry, imagined holding one in my hand, small and round and light as air. "They're not very big," I said.

I looked at Claude, wondering how many blueberries equaled his nearly three-year-old body, and if it would be possible to pick that many in a day. It was a math problem I was determined to solve. "How many pounds do you think Claude weighs?"

Patrick snorted like it was a dumb question, but

turned to our mom anyway. "How much does Claude weigh, Mom?"

She shook her head. "I have no idea what you two are talking about."

"Blueberries," I said. "A summer job."

Mom pulled her eyes away from the tumbleweeds long enough to squint at the newspaper spread across the floor. She said, "Where did you find that?"

"What?"

"That newspaper. It can't be current. Those berry farms stopped hiring kids years ago. Did you get it at Second Time Around? In one of those free piles by the door?"

Patrick pulled the paper close to his face. Then he turned it around and pointed to the date on the top. "It's this year. It's this week, even. Look!"

"Well, is it a real newspaper? Or is it one of those strange free things you kids are always picking up everywhere?"

"I'd watch out for Missy," my brother said, tucking the strange free newspaper behind his back.

"And I'd watch out for Patrick."

"And it's a farm. There's a farmer—"

"That place is—" my mom shook her head. "I remember back when I was a kid. There was some sort of dispute or something. They stopped hiring pickers, or sold half of the farm. I don't know the details." She turned back to the TV. "Anyway."

"What does that mean?" I demanded.

"What?"

"When you say 'anyway' like that. What does it mean? You always do it. And we never know what it means." I'm not stupid. I knew exactly what it meant, but I wanted her to have to say it. To emphasize the seriousness of the situation, I yanked off my 3-D glasses and glared across the room.

My mom looked down at Claude, twisting and turning on her lap. He was named after her name, which is Claudia. "Mr. Claude is having another dream," she said.

She said this out loud, but she wasn't really saying it to Patrick or me. More like to an imaginary adult—my mother's own imaginary friend who seemed to have moved in right after our dad moved out.

I turned to Patrick. He had gone limp. He sat hunched over his newsprint-smeared hands but I could tell he wasn't seeing them.

I knew what he was seeing. He was seeing the second half of the summer, dragging on like the first. He was seeing September, when he'd be starting as a freshman at the gigantic high school. He was seeing brand-new clothes from the mall, bought with money he'd earned through work in the blueberry field. He was seeing it all disappear with our mom's *anyway.*

"There's got to be another job for you," Mom said, softening a little. "Mowing lawns or walking dogs. Patrick, bring me the paper."

Patrick didn't move and his ears were turning a strange mix of red and purple.

So I said, "Mom, there's not," even though I knew he hated when I spoke for him. But what else could I do? His ears—I was afraid they would pop off.

I said, "Seriously, this isn't fair. All we want is to earn money so we don't look stupid at school next year."

"You kids never look stupid."

"How do you know? You don't know how it is. Look at us, Mom. We look as stupid as this ratty old carpet."

My voice was so loud it woke Claude, who sat up, stretched his chubby arms, and shouted, "Cats!"

Claude's dreams are usually about cats, which is funny because we don't even have one. When he wakes, we often go searching for his dream cats, peeking behind curtains and underneath chairs. But not right then. Because right then, a funny whistling sound was in the room, and it seemed to be coming from Patrick. I looked him up and down. The noise, I finally figured out, had to do with his nostrils, which were flaring, which led me to believe he was either about to explode or cry.

I turned back to my mother, expecting to see the People-Are-Suffering-So-Stop-Your-Complaining look that always followed any sort of conversation about new clothes and summer camps. Instead, I saw something new. She had gone limp, too.

The room was quiet until Claude made a wet bubbling sound. Usually Claude's bubbling sounds made everyone laugh, but at that moment, no one moved. Claude looked around, surprised. "But I funny," he said.

I felt bad about what I'd said to my mom. I really did. But I knew this: I would have felt a lot worse if Patrick had started to cry, right there on the bad living room carpet.

I picked up the strange little newspaper and held it out to my mom. "Can't you at least call?" I wished I still had my glasses on. I couldn't look her in the eye.

"No, Missy," she said. It was one of those times she said my name like it wasn't my name. Like if I were named Catherine or Gwen, she would still have called me Missy. Little Missy. Missy Smarty. "And you can go to your room."

CHAPTER 2

IF IT HADN'T BEEN FOR PATRICK BEING EMBARRASSED by our secondhand look, I never would have noticed. I'm like that, though. Something needs to be pointed out before I see it clearly. Which is why the 3-D glasses come in handy. Plus, I have my two best friends, Constance and Allie, and they don't seem to care where anyone's jeans come from.

Patrick has always liked nice things. My mother says that when he was a baby, he liked to look at furniture catalogs. My dad is like that, too. I, on the other hand, don't even like sitting on furniture.

Patrick gets nervous when we shop at Value Village or Second Time Around because he's afraid we'll run into someone we know. "Why should we care?" I ask. "They're doing the same thing we are."

He never has an answer to this logic of mine except, "You just wait, Missy. Someday you'll understand."

After I got sent to my room, I sat on my bed for three minutes. Then I decided to make my bed, just in case Mom came in to yell at me. I pulled the sheets up tight and fluffed the pillow. I smoothed the bedspread until it was perfectly flat.

On the other side of the room was Claude's bed, which wasn't a real bed, but something called a toddler bed. Mom hadn't gotten around to making it yet, so without even being asked, I straightened his sheets and fluffed his pillow, too. I even folded his little kitty-cat pajamas and tucked them in his top drawer. Then I opened the bedroom door, just a crack, to hear what was going on down the hall. But they either weren't talking or they knew I would be trying to listen, so they were torturing me by whispering. That's what happens in a family—everyone learns everyone else's Very Worst Thing.

My Very Worst Thing was being left out. Left out of the fun or discussion or even the fight. So with nothing to do but stare at my face in the mirror—an activity I endured until my eyebrows started looking creepy—I decided to play Intruder.

Intruder is a game I invented right after my dad moved out. It goes like this: You are all alone and you hear a strange noise in the house. Intruder! Quick, you crawl underneath your bed and you camouflage yourself to look like a pile of junk. The intruder will come in, searching for stuff to steal. When he looks underneath your bed, he will see junk. He might poke it even but will quickly realize there is nothing worth stealing.

It's not so easy, becoming a camouflaged pile of junk, and I had spent months collecting just the right objects:

My Princess Castle and all its parts, saved from last summer's giveaway pile.

My toy horses that I don't play with anymore but still want to keep.

This doll I got for my fifth birthday—she hums when she's happy and cries when she's hungry, except she doesn't do either anymore because of no batteries.

A silk fairy costume, which, due to an embarrassing flying experiment, has only one rainbow-sparkled wing.

And the most useful item for playing Intruder: Claude's outgrown baby blanket, the one with the hole in the middle, just right for covering my face and not suffocating.

The hardest body part to camouflage is feet, because no matter how you try to disguise them, sticking-up feet look exactly like sticking-up feet. I'd finally come up with the best solution ever: my mother's garden boots. They were big enough to go over my feet and flop down at odd angles, looking exactly like they'd been tossed carelessly underneath the bed. Every once in a while my mother asks, "Has anyone seen my garden boots?" but I usually only feel bad for a few minutes, and besides, it's not like she doesn't have other shoes to wear.

I had just arranged everything in perfect random order, slipped on the garden boots, and placed my feet in their thrown-under-the-bed position when I heard a noise at the door. I quick grabbed Claude's old baby blanket and draped it over my face, my heart beating so hard in my chest I was sure someone would hear it. That's the thing about Intruder—even when you know it's just a game, it sort of doesn't feel like it.

"Missy?"

Through the baby blanket hole I saw Patrick's feet in the doorway.

I flung off all my Intruder junk and crawled out from underneath the bed. "What's happening? Am I in trouble?"

Patrick shook his head. His ears were still red, but not so purple, and he was smiling. "She did it."

"What?"

"She called the blueberry people."

"What? Really?"

"Yeah, after you left."

He stepped into my room with his slight Patrick limp, on account of his right leg being just a tiny bit longer than his left. In his hand was a rolled-up catalog. "She called the number. She talked to a lady."

"Wow," I said. "I don't believe it."

"I know." He sat on the edge of my bed, and I plopped down next to him.

"What did she say? The lady?"

"I don't know exactly. Mom just listened and nodded her head for a long time. She asked about the stuff that happened there, years ago. The trouble."

"What trouble, Patrick? What kind of trouble?" My spine was suddenly tingly, the way it got before something big was going to happen.

Patrick shrugged. "Some sort of fight, I guess. Between the brothers."

"What brothers?"

"I don't know, Missy. The farmers, probably. They divided the farm so everything is all right now."

"So can we go?"

"She said that Bev told her they opened it up to kids last week—"

"Who is Bev?"

"The lady she was talking to."

"So can we go? Or are we too late? Do they already have all the pickers?"

"No, we're not too late. They still need more kids. But they had to postpone because of the weather. The lady said to wait for a few days of sun."

I glanced out the window. Gray skies and splats of rain against the glass. "But Mom said yes?"

"I guess she did, Missy."

I still couldn't believe it. "So did she say a bunch of rules?"

"That's the funny thing. She just looked at me the way she does. You know?"

I nodded. Mom had a look like a laser beam that could burn warning messages straight into a brain. But the laser-beam warning usually came with a long list of words.

"It was like—" he shook his head.

"What?"

"It was like I was a grown-up. And she didn't need to say all the usual stuff."

We sat in silence, trying to understand this new thing. I looked him up and down. To me he still looked like skinny Patrick. The only thing different was the enormous red pimple on his chin.

"What about me?" I asked finally. "Did she say anything about me?"

"She said we'd need to stick together out there."

I rolled onto my back and kicked my feet in the air. "I did it! And you owe me a big fat thank-you." When I heard Patrick open his catalog I sat back up. He was looking at the end section, with all the pictures of beach things.

"She cried though."

"What?"

"Mom cried. Because of what you said."

"What did you do?"

Patrick shrugged. "I didn't know what to do, so I just sat there. Claude patted her back and then she sort of laughed. But still, she seemed sad."

For once, I didn't know what to say. I had made my mother cry? Just thinking about it turned my stomach into a twisted knot. I wondered if I was having an appendicitis attack, brought on by stress and sorrow. I hoped so. Then she would have to forgive me.

"The first thing I'm going to buy," Patrick said, studying his catalog, "is a pair of swimming shorts, the long kind. For the lake."

Even as I said, "Uh-huh," I wondered if he would really be brave enough to show up at the lake. The summer before, right after he'd been nicknamed Praying Mantis

Boy, he woke up with a sick stomach every lake day. "Anyway," I added, "when are we going to have time for the lake? We'll be too busy picking blueberries."

"Weekends," he said. "Dad weekends."

"Uh-huh," I said again. Dad weekends were about a lot of things, but never about the lake. Mostly they were about Dad and Dad's girlfriend, Tessa. About fixing up Dad's new old house and "getting to know Tessa better."

Patrick flipped through the catalog's heavy pages filled with photographs of teenagers playing in the surf and sand. Their teeth were all shiny white. Their hair had streaks of sun. "Forty-two cents a pound," he said.

"And a prize," I reminded him.

"What are you going to buy, Missy?"

I studied the pages and wondered: Could you buy hair like that? A group of laughing friends? A perfect afternoon at the beach?

"Maybe those shorts," I said finally, because I couldn't give voice to the other secret wishes. I could barely let myself think them. "The ones with the little flower stitched on the pocket."

CHAPTER 3

DAD WASN'T SO SURE THE BLUEBERRIES WERE A good idea, even though Patrick brought the calculator that weekend and punched numbers like a crazy math genius. It was Sunday afternoon, after lunch, and we were counting down to our three o'clock going-home time.

"Dad," Patrick started in again, "you always say that if we want more than you can provide we need to work for it. And now we've found a job, but you're saying no."

Tessa cleared her throat. "Ted," she said, "the kids have been making good points all weekend. It's a summer job, a learning experience. Like camp would be."

I looked at Patrick. His eyes were wide. Tessa hardly ever spoke up in family discussions.

"Yes, it's a summer job," Dad said slowly. "But so are other things. Like, well, mowing lawns."

"Mom already called the field," I said quickly. "There's a lot of supervision, if that's what you're afraid of. And Tessa's right. It's just like camp."

Even though she'd been hanging around for way too long, it was the first time I'd said her name out loud, and it sort of stuck in my throat like I imagined a hairball or a fish bone would.

Dad shook his head. "I'm not afraid. I just didn't think kids were allowed to do that kind of thing anymore. Child labor or something."

"This is more like an experience," Patrick said. "Like Tessa said. It's what the lady told Mom, too."

Dad's face got tight, like a balloon with one too many puffs of air. "I just want what's best for the two of you," he said finally.

"Sure, Dad. We know." Patrick still believed everything Dad said.

"Right," I started in a mocking voice, but then nothing more came out. Words swirled around in my head—all the mean things I wanted to say. But suddenly, I couldn't put them together. And then my heart constricted. Was I having a heart attack? At twelve? Could bottled-up words be choking my heart?

Dad, not noticing my sudden medical emergency, cleared his throat cheerily. "Okay, listen! How about a frozen treat?"

My dad works for a company that makes ice-cream bars. It's how he met Tessa, less than a year after he moved out of our house. Mom and Dad said it was both their decision to split up, that they just couldn't get along as married people, but they'd always get along as our parents. Claude had just learned to walk.

"Like that makes any sense," I said at the time. "What about Claude? This might stunt his growth." To which they had no response except, "It will all work out, Missy," and, "It's for the best."

What I really wanted to say was this: Claude's only had one Christmas with all of us being a family. One birthday. One month of walking on his own two feet. But I could barely even say those words to myself.

So Dad found himself a mess of a house—a "fixer-upper" he called it. And we got this thing called a Parenting Plan, which told us when we got to be with Dad and when we got to be with Mom, and everything felt weird, especially since Claude didn't spend the whole weekend with us at Dad's yet, and then there was Tessa, who he met at some weird frozen-treat convention for weird frozen-treat people. And that's when ice cream stopped tasting so good to me.

Dad pulled two boxes from the freezer and placed them in the middle of the table. He pointed at the one with a picture of a sombrero-wearing banana. "Something new we're testing," he said. The banana appeared to be dancing. There was a crazy balloon coming from its mouth, with the words: *Banana Amarillo!*

"Why is the banana saying that?" My voice had found its way back to me.

"It's the name of the product."

I picked up the other box, happy to see that it was the only thing I could still choke down: ice-cream sandwiches. There are no tricks or surprises in an ice-cream sandwich. No crazy packages that try to convince you of something. Just pure vanilla ice cream sandwiched between two soft chocolate wafers.

Because he knew Dad wanted him to, Patrick opened the dancing banana box. "Bananas can't dance," I warned him. "They do not wear hats or speak. Never eat anything so full of lies." Then I pushed back my chair and marched out of the kitchen, making gagging sounds with every step. *Ghaagh, ghaagh, ghaagh.*

Because sound effects are often more accurate than words.

Even though dramatic exits are thrilling in the

moment, they mean you miss out on all the exciting things that happen after you leave. And also you miss your ice-cream treat. Luckily, I had Patrick to fill me in. So what came next, after I'd *ghaaghed* out of the room, was this: They had a fight. A real fight. The first fight in the history of Ted and Tessa.

"I can't believe I missed it," I whispered.

"I know. She called him spineless."

We were in Patrick's bedroom and I was sitting on his bed, gulping down the melting mess of ice-cream sandwich he'd smuggled up for me. Through a mouthful of cold vanilla-and-chocolate goodness I said, "Well, he *is* spineless."

"Shut up, Missy. He's our dad."

"I know. He's our spineless dad."

Patrick shoved the last of his weekend clothes into his backpack. "Anyway, we're picking blueberries this summer."

"I already knew that. Mom already decided."

"But Dad said it was okay, so now it's official."

I licked my fingers clean. "I don't care what he says. He's just a weekend dad. He has no rights during the week."

"That's not true."

"It's true for me," I said.

"Well, that's just stupid."

"I'm stupid, then. But I'm not spineless."

"You need to watch your mouth, Missy."

He didn't say it in a mean way so I said, "I know."

Patrick liked Dad weekends. He liked the color of his bedroom walls and the fact that all his bedding matched—sheets and pillowcases and bedspread. He liked that the hardwood floors had been sanded smooth and were now the color of honey.

I liked the bedding, too, but I never slept as well as I did at home in the room I shared with Claude, who breathed too loud, giggled in his sleep, and shouted out words like, "No!" and "Pee-pee!" and, of course, "Cat!" And I've always liked having carpet on the floor, even if it is bad green and worn out by too many feet.

Patrick slung his bag over his skinny shoulder. "Come on, Stupid."

I laughed. "Coming, Spineless."

I rode in the backseat of the car, staring at the small patch of scalp beginning to peek through the wavy black hair of my father's head. If it had been an ordinary day—a day with no fighting or stomping up the stairs—I would have said something to him about it. Something like, "Hey, Dad, you probably don't know this but you have a bald spot the size of a silver dollar. And your scalp is all shiny and white underneath."

I turned my attention to the back of Patrick's head. Except for not having a bald spot, it could have been my father's. It made me wonder what the back of my own head looked like.

I put on my 3-D glasses and stared out the window. With the world framed in that perfect black border, I was able to slip into the foggy little dream I slipped into every Sunday Dad drove us home. It only lasted the length of our street, but it gave me such an awful good feeling, I couldn't stop. I pretended we were all going home to stay.

CHAPTER 4

IT RAINED THE NEXT DAY AND THE DAY AFTER THAT, too. While Mom taped thin strips of yellow paint samples to the living room wall, Patrick and I searched the sky for a break in the clouds.

We waited for the five o'clock weather report, and even rode our bikes to the library to consult a thing called *The Farmer's Almanac,* which made me an expert on the different natural disasters that might occur at any moment, including earthquakes, flash floods, sinkholes, and volcanic eruptions, which are still a real thing, especially to people like me, who have lived their entire life in the shadow of Mount Saint Helens.

Even though I still didn't know what a blueberry

plant looked like, I imagined those poor berries out in a field, small and green and wrinkled with cold. The worst part was wondering if this weather delay would make Mom change her mind, so I did everything possible to prove I was worthy of my first job.

Without being asked, I made my bed and cleaned my room, including Claude's side. I played hide-and-seek with Claude, even when he didn't want to. I did not mock Patrick when he made his smelly protein drink for breakfast, or when he lifted weights in front of the bathroom mirror. I did not ask to ride my bike around the neighborhood or visit my friends Constance and Allie, not once. And I folded pile after pile of laundry, and even tried to start the washing machine with a load of Claude's clothes that were disgustingly crusted with pieces of honey toast and chunks of banana.

The one thing I did not do was apologize to my mom. The words were there, always on the end of my tongue, but they would not come out, no matter how bad I wanted them to.

But Mom didn't seem to mind. She thanked me for helping with Claude, and didn't get too mad when the washing machine got clogged with suds because I hadn't read the instructions on the detergent label. And she even remembered when it was Packing Day.

"Aren't you going to Constance's house this afternoon?" she asked. I'd been sitting in front of the window, searching the dark clouds for a glimmer of light.

"What?"

"Isn't it Packing Day?"

"I guess," I said.

"Do you want me to drive you over there? It looks like it might pour again."

I shrugged. "I could ride my bike. If I go."

Mom shot me her laser eyes, but this time, instead of trying to put something into my brain, it was like she was trying to suck something out. "Is everything okay?"

"What?"

"Are you and your friends getting along?"

"Of course," I said quickly. "Why wouldn't we be?"

"No reason. Sometimes things just change."

"What do you mean change? No one is changing, Mom. Ever."

Mom smiled. "Then you'd better get over there. Packing Day is halfway over."

I laughed. "Not when Constance is packing." I went to my room and grabbed a sweatshirt, then took my 3-D glasses from the special top drawer. I slipped them in my pocket.

It was nice to be on my bike. Even though everyone

complains about how much it rains in the Pacific Northwest, the air is always fresh here, and the grass and trees are a bright and cheery green. I pumped my legs as fast as they would go and felt the good damp air fill my lungs. The tires made swishing sounds as they sliced through the murky brown puddles.

I turned the corner of our development and pedaled past the entrances to two other developments. Both Constance and Allie lived in the third development down from me, exactly seven minutes by bike.

Constance's mother met me at the front door. "Where have you been, Miss Missy? I'm no help and poor Allie is about to lose her mind."

"Sorry," I said. "I lost track of time." I walked down the hall and stood quietly in the bedroom doorway, studying my two best friends. They were so different from each other—Constance, like a three-year-old or a chipmunk, constantly darting from one shiny object to the next, and Allie, more like one of those panting dogs in Scotland, the kind obsessed with herding sheep into neat little pens.

Allie, who was sitting on the edge of the bed, saw me first. "Missy! It's about time!" She rolled her eyes at Constance, the pile of clothes and empty suitcase in the middle of the floor. "Every time I put something in she takes it out!"

Packing Day had started two summers before, when Allie and Constance first signed up for the same sleepaway camp on the east side of the Cascade Mountains, where it is a guaranteed summer with no rain. They tried to get me to go with them, but my parents said it was too far away and too expensive. I know Packing Day was supposed to help me feel like I was a part of things, and it had worked that way before. But standing there, I just felt dangly and useless. Still, I tried to sound cheerful when I plopped down next to Allie and said, "Okay, what can I do?"

Constance, with a furry pink slipper in her hand, wandered around the room. "I need a theme," she said. "To help me get started."

Allie jumped up. "I told you. The theme is *summer camp*." She grabbed the furry slipper from Constance's hand and tossed it aside. Then she crouched next to the pile of clothes and pawed through it. Soft, wispy things flew through the air. "You don't need anything like any of this. You need shorts. T-shirts. One sweatshirt for chilly nights. Where's your underwear?"

I slid off the bed, joined Allie at the clothing pile, and dug around until I found a black velvet cap. "You'll need a hat," I said, placing it on my head. "Even I know that and I've never been to camp."

Allie snatched away the cap. "No velvet at summer camp!" She dug out a pair of khaki shorts and dropped it in the suitcase. "There. Do *not* remove. And find more like it."

Constance reached into the pile and pulled out a bathing suit top. It still had the tags. She placed it in the suitcase, right next to the khaki shorts. Then Allie found a pink bra and said, "Where are your others? You'll need at least two more bras." Which made Constance sigh dramatically.

"Well, thank goodness I don't have to worry about that," I said, my voice a little too loud to be real.

My friends had both started wearing bras during the school year, and they always acted like it was such a big deal. Even though I didn't want one or need one, I still felt a little bit left out by the whole thing. I took out my 3-D glasses and slipped them on. "Don't forget these."

Constance and Allie, perfectly framed, exchanged a look. "What?" I said.

"I'm not bringing my glasses to camp," Allie said quietly.

Constance said, "I'm not either."

I stared from one to the other. Then I touched the Spectacular Button on the right side of the frame. It was an actual button, midnight blue, glued on with Allie's mom's hot glue gun. "But we always take our glasses with us." I hated how my voice was an embarrassing mix of angry and whiny. I pushed the button again, as if it hadn't worked the first time.

"I see something now . . . no, wait—" I pushed the button a third time. When I spoke again, it was in a robot voice. Which I know is dorky, but sometimes necessary to prove a point.

"In-Spectacular-Vision-I-See-That-You-Two-Are-Very-Grown-Up-Now-That-You-Go-to-Sleepaway-Camp-and-Also-Wear-Bras."

Constance tried to interrupt. "Missy—"

"No—Wait!" I pushed the Spectacular 3-D Button again. "Perhaps-We-Should-Also-Discuss-Marriage-and-Careers."

Allie's face turned red—it does that when she gets mad. But Constance just laughed, her perfect Constance laugh. She reached over to her dresser and this time pulled out her own pair of 3-D glasses. She unfolded the plastic stems and slipped them on. The lenses had been removed, just like mine, but instead of colored markers and construction paper, Constance had decorated her frames with pipe cleaners and rainbow glitter-glue. She touched her Spectacular Button, which was purple.

"There," she said. "You're right, Missy. Now I see it all clearly, too."

The three of us had seen our first 3-D movie together at the start of fifth grade, and when we'd walked out of the theater, bent over and laughing, had decided to keep our glasses on the entire day. But doing that gave us headaches, so we took out the lenses. And that's when we made the most amazing discovery of all time—that we could actually see a new dimension just by wearing the frames. We could see through everything fake and phony. We could see what was *Spectacular.*

So we spent the rest of that afternoon decorating them and then wore them to school the next day. And we made a pact—to have them with us at all times.

So what if the other kids made fun of us? So what? Because, as our motto goes: You Never Know When You Need to See the World Clearly.

I stared at Constance and she stared at me. We both smiled, standing there and Seeing the World Clearly. Then we turned to Allie.

"Okay, you guys." She reached into her backpack and pulled out her glasses, which were also decorated, but with scraps of colorful fabric, like a perfect miniature patchwork quilt. Her Spectacular Button was small and cute and shiny black.

"Whew," I said, trying to make a joke of it. "For a minute I thought we were goners."

But the truth was I knew we still weren't seeing the same thing. For the first time ever, our Spectacular Buttons were not in synch. No one said it, but I could tell.

Later, while the oven warmed up, we sat on the counter and kicked our feet in rhythm. I was about to tell them about my summer job (I'd even waited for dramatic effect), but the longer I went without saying anything, the harder it became.

Then Constance's mother walked in wearing a purple skirt and earrings that dangled to her shoulders. During the week she had a regular job in an office, but on some nights and weekends she told people's fortunes with these things called tarot cards. She worked from a velvet-covered table set up in the back of a small bookstore, and people came from all over to have their futures told by her. She was that good.

"Oh my goodness! Does this mean you're ready to go?" Constance's mother raised her arms in a victory pose.

"Well, not exactly," said Allie.

"There are three things in her suitcase," I added, imagining Constance for four weeks wearing nothing but the same bathing suit top, khaki shorts, and pink bra.

Constance said, "We got hungry, Mom. We're taking a break."

Constance's mother dropped her arms and glanced at the clock. "I wish I could give you girls a reading for your upcoming summer adventures, but I'm running late. Allie, honey, make sure my girl gets packed."

"I will," Allie promised.

"And Missy, honey," she blew me a kiss, "you come and visit me, any weekend. I'll give you a reading then."

"Okay." I giggled. She was outrageously fantastic.

"I'll be so lonely without you all!" She swept out of the kitchen, blowing more kisses, and leaving the air behind her smelling spicy and sweet, like fresh oranges and soap from China. The front door slammed and then it opened again. "And don't forget to take the plastic off the pizza before you cook it!"

"Okay!" we called back together. The door slammed again.

Constance said, "She always forgets. About the plastic." Then she expertly removed the pizza from the box, tore off the plastic wrap, and checked the thermometer one last time before popping the pizza in the oven.

"Your mom is the best," I said.

Constance shrugged. "I just wish she could cook."

Allie and Constance were both still wearing their glasses so I put mine back on, too. Maybe I'd been wrong before. Maybe our Spectacular Buttons would work the way they were supposed to. I let out a relieved breath; the world looked nearly right again.

Constance set the timer for the pizza. "Fifteen minutes. What should we do?"

"Pack," Allie said. "We should pack."

But Constance was already picking up the phone. "Let's call Ben. We can pretend to be someone else."

"Who would we pretend to be?" I asked. "And why would we call him?" I knew the answer to that second question. Along with wearing bras, something else had changed for my two friends. They had developed a crush. On the same boy. Ben Masterson. They even had a notebook called the *BM Book* and in it they chronicled everything about him: what he wore to school, what he ate for lunch, where his classes were, and also the first and last numbers of his locker combination. They were still spying on him for the middle.

When they'd first come up with the book, I was quick to point out that BM also stood for bowel movement, which means poop, which I thought was funny, but they did not.

While I stared at the pizza timer, Constance handed the phone to Allie, who punched in his number and held the phone to her ear. After a moment, she hung up. "Message," she said.

Constance said, "Maybe we should leave a real message for him. Tell him we're going away for camp. Ask him what he's doing this summer. Like if he goes to the lake or something like that."

"That's so grown up of you," I said. "I liked it better when you just made farting noises and hung up."

"Missy! We only did that once!"

"Twice," I said.

Allie picked up the phone again. "I'm going to do it. Only I'm going to tell him my name is Allison."

"Why?"

Allie glanced at Constance before turning to me. She put down the phone. "I just decided. I'm going to start using my real name this summer. And probably next school year, too."

"What?" I noticed that Constance didn't seem surprised by Allie's news. "Why?"

Allie shrugged. "It's my real name."

"What about you, Missy?" Constance said.

"What about me? Missy is my name."

Allie said, "Missy is a nickname."

"My parents had me when they were young. They didn't know the difference. They thought it was cute. Missy McKenzie." The picture of my parents, young and happy and naming me as a baby . . . I couldn't look at it that closely.

I yanked off my 3-D glasses and my friends did the same. We all looked sort of startled without them.

"Then you could be anyone," Constance said finally. "That's *so* exciting!"

"Right," Allie agreed. "You could go by Marsha. Or Melissa."

My throat tightened as I twiddled with the timer. Fifteen minutes while you're waiting for a pizza and your friends are being stupid is just about the longest time in the world. I said, "You guys haven't asked me what I'll be doing this summer."

"Are you doing something, Missy?"

I shrugged. Why was it suddenly hard to talk? I wanted so badly to tell them about the blueberry field—about Patrick finding the ad and about how I made my mom cry, and about Dad and Tessa's fight over the whole thing, and about how we were waiting, waiting, waiting for a few days of sunshine. But all I could say was, "I might get a job."

"A job? A real job?" Allie's eyes lit up. "Are we actually old enough to do that?" Even though I didn't wear a bra or have a crush on a boy, I'd stepped up a rung on Allie's maturity ladder. They were both all over me then, asking a million questions, but the funny thing was, I sort of didn't want to tell them any more.

So I said, "It's not definite yet. I'm just looking in the newspaper. I'll write and tell you if it happens."

I had never kept something big from my friends before, and I didn't know what to do next. So without them seeing me, I turned the knob on the timer, making it go off five minutes before it was supposed to.

No one seemed to care that the pizza was a tiny bit frozen in the middle. The crusts were delicious anyway, and we ate slowly, trying to make it last, and everything felt almost normal by the time I had to leave.

My friends walked me to the door. They handed me the *BM Book*. "If you see him," they said, "write it down. Everything. And write to us, too. Everything."

"I will," I promised.

"Make sure you write 'Allison' on the envelope," Allie reminded me.

I didn't ask them again if they were bringing their glasses to camp. We all wore them when we hugged good-bye, but I sort of wished we hadn't. In Spectacular 3-D it was easy to see the unbearable truth: that this might be our very last time of wearing them together.

CHAPTER 5

FINALLY THERE WAS A DAY OF PURE SPARKLING sunshine. Followed by another. And another. We begged Mom to call the blueberry people.

"We'll open the fields first thing Monday," the lady told her. "Send them with a sack lunch and make sure they dress in layers. It can be chilly in the mornings."

So on Sunday night, before I went to bed, I pulled out clothes and arranged them on my chair according to appropriate layering order. It took a long time to fall asleep because I was afraid the alarm wouldn't go off, or that maybe I hadn't turned it on right.

But the alarm did go off, just as it was supposed to, and with those first few beeps I scrambled out of bed, pulled on my layers, and ran to get Patrick, who was already up and dressed. He smiled at me and I smiled at him. The feeling in my stomach was bigger than the first day of a new school year.

Mom stood at the kitchen counter, making sandwiches for our lunches. Claude was slumped on the floor, still half asleep. "Morning, Mom," I said. I went straight to the cupboard for the cereal while Patrick got out the milk.

"Morning, Missy." She nodded at my bowl of cereal. "Honey, when you're done with that would you take my coffee to the car? And Patrick, maybe you could take Claude and get him buckled in?" I finished my cereal in three bites.

I'd never been up so early in the summer and was surprised by how perfectly still the world could be. Patrick carried Claude across the grass, so his feet wouldn't get wet from the dew. Mom came out with our lunches. I took the lunches and handed her the coffee, which I'd balanced on the hood of the car. Patrick climbed into the front seat while I sat in the back, shoulder-to-shoulder with my baby brother, cozy in his pajamas and smelling slightly of pee.

Mom hadn't taken the time to comb her hair; she had just pulled it back in a tight, messy ponytail. She held her coffee in one hand and maneuvered through the empty morning streets with the other. I closed my eyes, smelled the good coffee smell, and pretended I was a grown-up woman on her way to work. I would drink coffee in the car, too. I would drive with one hand and hum under my breath.

I wondered if my mom ever missed going to work in an office. She used to wear such nice clothes. Skirts so straight they were called pencil skirts, with little matching jackets and shiny shoes that clicked across the kitchen floor every morning. She had quit her job just before Claude was born and started her own accounting business, working from a desk shoved in the farthest corner of the kitchen. During her busy time, when people need their taxes done, she's permanently hunched over her desk, and she never has to dress up anymore.

"I want boo-berries," Claude mumbled through his fingers. "We get boo-berries."

Mom glanced over her shoulder. "Claude, this is a job for Missy and Patrick. You get to come home with me and play with your toys."

"You can pick blueberries when you're bigger." I gave his arm a tickle, then leaned forward in my seat. "How much longer, Patrick?"

"I'm not really sure." His answer made my mom sigh.

I slumped down in my seat and tried not to worry about what a sigh like that might mean.

On that drive to the blueberry field, the world started to shift. I noticed it first with the houses. The farther we got from town, the more space grew between them, until there were no developments anymore, just houses standing bravely on their own. Patrick suddenly pointed to a sign that said Old Farm Road. "There, Mom. Turn there."

I pressed my forehead against the cool window and stared hard. *This?* I thought in amazement. *This has always been here? All this land, just outside our town?*

Old Farm Road was narrow and bumpy with a wall of pine trees on one side and wide-open fields on the other. In the middle of the fields, cows ate grass and horses leaned against faded barns to soak up the first rays of morning sun. "Look, Claude," I said, pointing. "Look at the horses."

"Cats," he said, sucking his fingers.

Next to each old-fashioned farmhouse were these large, round satellite dishes. Stark and white, they looked like they'd been dropped straight from outer space, and were pretty much the only sign that we hadn't magically traveled back in time.

I tried to imagine what might be happening behind all the different walls. Were farm kids churning butter from the cream of the cows they'd just milked? Were they wearing overalls? Or were they just like us, lying on the couch in their Spider-Man pajamas, eating Fruit Loops, and watching the cartoons that those big white satellite dishes had sucked from the sky? I stared at each house, hoping for a glimpse inside, but I couldn't tell anything from the dark, curtained windows.

Patrick looked down at his directions. "We should be getting close, Mom." And then he sat up straight, pressed his face to the window, and pointed excitedly. "I think that's the farm, Mom! Turn there!"

I followed Patrick's pointing finger to a white wooden board with BLUEBERRIES printed in fading red paint. As Mom turned into the drive, the tires made a loud crunching sound on gravel. The car dipped and bumped and curved until we came to a long, flat brown house. I thought about the ad in the newspaper, with Patrick's fingers smearing the ink. This was the place behind those smeared words.

Even before the car had completely stopped, Patrick was lunging for the door. "The blueberries must be down that road," he said breathlessly.

Mom stopped him with her arm. "Wait a minute, Mister." She eyed the place suspiciously. "I'm not just going to drop you off here. Where is everyone?"

I unbuckled my seat belt and climbed over Claude to get to the other window. On the side of the house was another white board, with red letters spelling the word OFFICE. I pointed. "Maybe over there?"

Mom sat a moment longer. Then she opened the car door. "Wait here." I watched her walk up to the office and rap on the window. I saw her lean her head down and motion back to our car.

Up front, Patrick squirmed. "I wish I could hear what they're saying." He sounded nervous. I was nervous, too. Nervous that our mother might change her mind, put the car in reverse, and then whisk us the wrong way along that country road, back to our world of beige-colored neighborhoods and tidy planting strips with miniature matching trees.

But Mom came back to the car smiling. She slid into her seat and said, "That very nice lady is Bev, the one I talked to on the phone. She's married to Moose, the farmer. The two of them run the farm together."

I said, "Moose? What kind of a name is Moose?" I was suddenly interested in names since, as I'd just dis-covered from my friends, mine wasn't a real one.

Patrick reached for the door handle. Mom put her hand on his shoulder. "Not so fast. You need to follow the road that leads to the fields. Follow it all the way down the hill. When you get to the bottom, you'll see that the field has been divided. One side belongs to Moose, and the other to his brother."

I looked across the gravel drive and saw a hedge, tall and thick as a wall.

"On the other side of the hedge is the brother's farm," Mom continued. "Always stay on this side of the hedge. It's planted there for a reason. Got it?"

"Got it," Patrick said.

I said, "What's the reason?"

"I told you, there was a fight out here, years ago. I don't know the details. Just stay on this side of the hedge and you'll be fine."

Suddenly realizing we were using a word he didn't know, Claude's head snapped up. He shouted, "Hedge! Hedge! Hedge!"

"It's like a bush, Mr. Claudio," I said, patting him on the arm. "It's just a plant."

"Scary," he whispered.

Mom held out our sack lunches. "Keep walking down the hill until you find the weigh station. There's a man named Al. He'll tell you everything else."

We grabbed the lunch sacks and bolted from the car before Mom could say another thing. But she managed to, anyway. Rolling down her window she gave us one last rule, which was her very own rule, which is always her rule, no matter what the situation.

"Remember!" she called. "You two stick together out there!"

CHAPTER 6

STARTING DOWN THE TIRE-TRACK ROAD, MY BROTHER and I walked in the faint morning shadow of the giant hedge. The word hedge didn't really seem to fit, since it was more like a dark and prickly prison wall than any sort of plant. "Claude was right," I said. "There is something scary about it."

At the bottom of the hill the road made a sharp curve, and at the end of that curve, the world opened to a brand-new place. The blueberry field.

My blueberry field. Because that's how I felt the moment I saw it. Love at first sight. Which I know is an embarrassing thing to say, but it is also just the truth.

"Patrick," I whispered. "This is where blueberries come from!"

"Of course, Missy." But I knew he was just as surprised as I was.

The delicate bushes looked like miniature trees, standing side-by-side in straight rows. The leaves on the bushes were oval in shape, tapered at the end, and the prettiest green I'd ever seen. Big bursts of purple-blue berries hung in clumps, more like party decorations than food. And the rows of plants went on forever, a perfect blanket of green and blue.

As I stood, breathing it all in, I learned the first secrets of blueberries—that plain air had an actual smell, and that quiet was an actual sound. I noticed, for the first time, how the fabric of my jeans rubbed against my legs, and also how the paper lunch sack felt in my hand, dry and crinkly. I learned right then that in a quiet place, I didn't have to speak every word that came through my head. I could just be quiet, too. All that I learned in an instant, without even knowing I learned it.

Patrick, for once, broke the silence. "Come on, Missy." He pulled on my arm. "Let's hurry." That's when I remembered what Mom had told us, about the man we were supposed to find.

We stepped quickly, kicking up dirt. "I think that's it," I said, pointing to the far end of the road, where a small shed was coming into focus. When we got close enough I could see that it was built on wheels, and open in the front, like a hot-dog stand at the beach. There was a man sitting inside.

The man was old, but not in the shriveled sort of way. The bulk of him filled out every inch of his plaid shirt and farmer overalls. He had a cup in his hand, a red plastic cup that fit over the top of a thermos. I smelled coffee. As the old man brought the red cup to his mouth, I noticed his hands. They were the biggest hands I'd ever seen, with fingers as thick and round as those pale German sausages that are creepy to look at but end up tasting pretty good.

The old man blew over his cup and squinted across the cloud of steam. "Well," he said finally, "how old are you kids?"

I cleared my throat, still staring at his enormous fingers. "Twelve," I said. "And my brother is almost fourteen."

"Can't he speak for himself?"

"Of course he can."

Patrick jabbed me with his elbow.

The old man chuckled, deep and low. "Okay, then. Hello and welcome to Moose G's Blueberry Farm. My name is Al. You don't have to call me Mister Al or anything like that. Just Al. Have you picked berries before?"

Patrick and I shook our heads. I was scared right

then, scared that the man would send us back up the hill and straight for home.

But he didn't. Instead, he set his plastic cup on the counter, next to a white scale with a chipped, round face. "Well," he said, "it's not as complicated as brain surgery. Or even wood shop. Do they still have that at school? Where you build things with wood?"

Patrick said yes while I said no and then we both said together, "I don't know."

The man picked up his cup again. "Well you should find out. It's a useful skill, working with your hands. Your hands are important. Hands and brain, working together. There is a connection. Like I said, this job is not as complicated as brain surgery, but it's not so easy, either. After a day or two your fingers will get the hang of it and you'll be ready to turn professional. If you keep your noses clean. You know what that means?"

Patrick said yes and I did, too, even though I wasn't exactly sure.

"It means stay out of trouble." Al sat back and looked at us so long and hard that I wanted to squirm. But I forced myself to stay frozen, so as not to appear like I had anything to hide. Because sometimes when someone stares at you like that, you start to think you've done something wrong, even when you haven't.

Finally Patrick said, "We will, sir."

"Don't call me sir. I'll send you home for that."

"Really?" I asked.

He motioned behind him with his frightening thumb. "See this hedge here?"

We nodded.

"It's there for a reason."

I said, "Our mom told us."

"So you know. You know to stay on the right side of this hedge here, no matter what anyone tells you. And if you see someone on your row who shouldn't be there, yell 'Row Hopper' real loud and I'll set the dogs on them."

I glanced around. Along with the idea of people sneaking up on me in the middle of those bushes, dogs made me extremely nervous. "Why would anyone be on my row?"

"What?" he barked. "Speak up."

"Why would anyone be on my row? If it's mine?"

"Oh, all sorts of crazy reasons." He settled back on his stool, like he had a good story to tell and the whole morning to tell it. "The biggest reason is to steal your berries. We used to have a Row Boss out here. Someone to sneak up on you kids and make sure you were keeping your noses clean. Can't do that anymore. We're just starting up again with pickers, after relying on the picking machine for years." He stared at us until I felt the need to say something.

"Okay," I said.

Nodding, he reached behind the counter and, with a clatter of metal, brought out two small buckets. He handed one to me and one to Patrick. The buckets were old tin coffee cans fitted with a long piece of wire, like a stretched-out coat hanger. The wire came together at the top to make a hook.

"These little ones here, these are your picking buckets. You slip this hook inside your belt buckle or a belt loop. That way both hands are free to pick. See?" And he showed us how to attach the hook at the end of the wire so that the can hung from our belt loops.

"Those are five-pound cans; they hold five pounds of berries. And those—" he pointed to the stacks of bigger metal buckets lined up all around the shed. "Those are your dumping buckets. You carry one of those out with you. When your little picking bucket gets full, you dump it into the big one. When the big one is full, come to me. I'll weigh it for you, write down the pounds you've picked, and give you a new big bucket."

I slipped the hook into my belt loop. The can rubbed against my thigh.

"The big buckets, when they're full, will weigh

anywhere from sixteen to twenty pounds, depending. So, let's see. What I need to do is write your names in my little book, here. That way I'll keep track of your pounds."

Al flipped open a notebook. The cover was stained and worn, and the blue lines of the paper had faded at the edges. "You're the first pickers out this morning. Your names will go on the very top of the list." The stubby pencil he pulled out disappeared between his sausage fingers. "Okay," he said, turning to Patrick. "Age before beauty."

I laughed.

"Patrick," my brother said.

"And what about you?"

"I'm Missy—no, wait." I took a deep breath. "Melissa."

Patrick snorted. But when I saw those extra-large fingers spell M-e-l-i-s-s-a in the blue-lined notebook, I didn't even care.

The old man named Al told us to stash our lunches in the coolers behind the shed. "You don't have any electronics with you, do you?"

"What?"

"Cell phones, a Walkman—"

"What's a Walkman?" I asked.

"It's what we used to call the musical device you kids plug into your ears."

"Oh, you mean like an iPod? Or a—"

"I don't care what you call it these days. It's not allowed out here. The only music allowed must come from an actual radio. With nothing plugged into your ears!"

"Okay," Patrick said. "We didn't bring anything like that."

"Good for you," the old man said. "Half the trouble in the world would be solved if we yanked those little wires out of ears. People need to know what's going on around them. They need to be able to communicate at least as well as a monkey. How's anyone supposed to do that if they always have their ears plugged into some space-age contraption? Can you explain that to me?"

I shook my head. "My mother says the same thing."

"Good for her," he said. "I hope you listen."

I cleared my throat. There was one more thing I had to know. "Can you tell us about the contest?"

He narrowed his eyes as he blew into his cup. "What contest?"

"In the paper. It said there would be a prize for the best picker."

He sipped on his coffee and shook his head. "That crazy fool. This is the craziest idea—" But then he stopped and sighed. "Well, I don't know any darn thing about it. But I do know about this. Work hard, pick clean, respect one another, and respect the bushes. That's what I know. That's what I've always known. I can't control the rest. Hard work is its own reward. That's the prize I care about. Understand?"

"Yes, sir," we both said.

"Start on row thirty-six. Walk down until you see the little wooden marker with the number thirty-six. One of you on either side. And call me Al."

We picked up our big metal buckets and had just started back down the tire-track road when Al called out after us, "And the biggest rule of all out here? Don't believe everything you hear!"

We kept our backs straight and didn't turn around. *"That was weird,"* I whispered when I was sure Al couldn't hear me. Then I got the giggles so hard Patrick had to hit me on the shoulder to make me stop.

I am not embarrassed to admit that my favorite stories always start with a step into the dark. Like Alice falling down her rabbit hole, or Lucy pushing her way through to the back of the wardrobe. Life could be absolutely normal and then, just one step later, absolutely not. I knew it was silly, but for a moment I wondered—could magic like that really happen? The air felt so heavy with unseen worlds it made me dizzy with hope.

The bushes were about a foot taller than me, lined up like soldiers, with branches so thick that they touched at the top, making the ends of each row look like entrances to tiny dark caves. Patrick went first, plunging into the opening that, like a giant mouth, swallowed him whole. When I ducked my head and stepped through the opening on the other side of the row, the branches slapped against my face like tiny wet hands. "Patrick! I can't even see!"

He didn't answer, but I could hear him clanging up ahead of me. I kept my head down and followed the clanging bucket sound, up the row until the bushes stopped hitting at me. When I straightened up, the back of my sweatshirt was soaked from dew, but I barely noticed because I was standing in the middle of a tunnel of green so thick, I could only see the sky as thin slivers of blue.

"Patrick!"

"Keep walking," he called. "It thins out a little farther up."

But I stayed where I was because blueberries, frosted blue and hanging in juicy fat clumps, were right in front of my face. I watched my fingers reach out and pick one. It made a tinny *pling* when it hit the bottom of the bucket hanging from my belt loop. *Food.*

Food was growing on a bush. I could see it. I could

reach out and touch it. I could touch it before anyone else and put it in my bucket. And what I put in my bucket would end up in a store for someone to buy and take home and cover with cream. Or drop into their cereal in the morning. I was responsible for putting blueberries on someone's table so they could finish their cornflakes and go off to work. I was suddenly a part of the world—the actual *world*. So I wasn't Alice or Lucy. My feet were on solid ground and it was just plain old earth. But even so, it was magic. Actual magic.

"We're picking blueberries, Patrick," I called. "We're actually picking blueberries that will be sold in a store."

The row between us was like a wall. From up ahead I heard the *pling, pling, pling* of berries covering the bottom of his bucket. "Of course, Missy," he answered in his matter-of-fact Patrick way. "What did you think?"

CHAPTER 7

AT FIRST, EVERYTHING WAS WET. THE TIPS OF MY fingers, white and wrinkled, looked like they'd soaked in a bath too long, and even my toes were numb from the dew-covered grass seeping through my shoes. The field was so quiet that all I heard was the rustle of branches, the sound of berries dropping in the bucket, and my own breathing.

But then all that changed, and I didn't even see it happening. Which is how it is with change. Things are one way and then—*WHAM*—they're another. Your parents are together and then—*WHAM*—they're not. Your friends wear 3-D glasses to school and then—*WHAM*—they are embarrassed when you pull yours from your pocket.

Too many *whams*.

But that's not the point. The point is: Suddenly, I wasn't cold, or damp even. And my fingers weren't wrinkled. And it wasn't quiet anymore—there were voices. And I had no idea how the sun had gotten hot like that, or when the voices had started.

"Hey, Patrick?" When he didn't answer I unhooked the little bucket from my belt loop and bent down to look for his feet. They weren't there. "Patrick?"

Your brother is across from you and then—*WHAM*—he's disappeared.

I walked down the row, peering through the gaps in branches. "Patrick!" I called, panic rising in my voice.

And then, from somewhere across the field, another voice echoed, "Patrick!" And then other voices chimed in, too, laughingly shouting out my brother's name. "Patrick! Patrick!"

Those voices.

I shut my mouth and continued quietly up the row, bending down every few steps to look for my brother's feet. And finally I saw them, planted on the other side, familiar and solid and real. I let out a breath I didn't know I'd been holding.

"Hey, Missy," he said.

"Patrick!" I squeezed between bushes and whispered in his ear, "I thought I lost you."

"The berries were better up here. Look—" he pointed to his big bucket. It was nearly full. "Why are you whispering?"

"I don't want anyone to hear me. Didn't you hear the voices?"

"No," he said. "But you don't have to whisper."

I sat right down in the middle of the row, shaded my eyes with my hand, and looked up. Patrick's neck was beginning to turn pink. I said, "Your mouth is purple."

He glanced down. "Yours isn't."

"I haven't eaten any."

"You should. They're good. But don't sit in the dirt, Missy. That's weird." He pointed to some scraggly weeds. "Sit there, next to the trunk."

"Trunk? Is it called a trunk?"

"I don't know. A stem?"

"It's thicker than a stem. A stem is like a flower. But a trunk is like a tree. And it's not like that, either."

"Then it's a strunk," Patrick said, and I laughed because ever since Dad moved out, Patrick hardly ever made silly jokes. His jokes didn't stop suddenly—more like a faucet of water slowing down, first to a trickle and then to an occasional drop. So I probably laughed harder than I needed to, at the drops. But I was always so glad when one came out.

Down in the shade, sitting on weeds and overturned earth, I reached for a berry hanging near the bottom of the bush. I'd eaten hundreds of blueberries in my life: in pancakes and muffins, in smoothies and pie. I'd eaten them without ever thinking about where they came from, how they grew, how they ended up in a store. But that first one in the field, straight from the bush and warm from the sun, was the sweetest, most real taste my mouth had ever known.

So I sat in the shade, eating every blueberry I could reach while Patrick worked hard to fill his bucket. I listened to the voices, calling from all over the field. I must have broken the silence spell by yelling for my brother.

They called out for each other's names. "Who are you?"

And answers came back like this: "Freddy Krueger! Which row are you on?"

They called out for information: "What time is it?"

And answers came back like this: "Time for you to get a watch!" Or "Same time it was yesterday at this time!"

They called out to complain and to joke and to tease. "Do you hear them now, Patrick?" I asked.

"Of course, Missy."

I wondered if Al had put us on rows all over the field to keep us apart. I wondered if it had anything to do with the hedge. "Well, I don't like it," I said quietly. "It's creepy."

"Just ignore them. Get back to work."

I got back to work, but I didn't ignore the voices. As I picked, I tried to sort them out—where they were in the field, how old they sounded, how many there were. They called one another names, like Earlobe, and Giant Johnny. Smith One, Smith Two, and Smith Three. There was a radio that turned on and off—or maybe several radios. It was hard to tell. And it was hard to tell what people were actually like, when you couldn't see their faces.

It was too easy to lie, all hidden like that.

CHAPTER 8

SOMETHING I LEARNED FROM MY MOM'S OLD COWBOY movies: When the sun is directly over your head, it's twelve o'clock noon. By noon, my big bucket was nearly halfway full and I had peeled down to my very last layer: cutoff shorts and a thin white T-shirt. When I touched the top of my head and it was as red-hot as a coiled stove burner set on high, I suddenly understood cowboy hats.

"When can we eat, Patrick?"

"What time is it even?"

"Noon. High noon. According to the sun." From some deep place in my stomach I felt a hollow rumble. "Can't we just go now?" The bushes were closing in on me, and I had to go to the bathroom so bad.

"Yeah," Patrick said. "Okay." I heard a clang and then the soft sound of berries tumbling from his small bucket to his big one. "There," he said. His voice was proud.

I grabbed my own big bucket and pushed back through my row, barely noticing how the branches slapped against my face and arms. The dew was long gone and my toes were dry. When I stepped out from the cover of the blueberry bushes I saw the giant hedge, just on the other side of the tire-track road. It made me shiver, even in the bright sunlight.

With stiff arms we carried our buckets. The grass that brushed against our legs was golden brown and smelled like bread baking in an oven. We found Al at the weigh station, perched on his stool and swatting at fat black flies with a rolled-up newspaper. I glanced at his hands. If this were that other kind of story, my favorite kind, Al would be part ogre.

Patrick hoisted his big bucket over to Al, who set it on the large white scale, making the thin red needle jump and shiver before it settled on a number. "Twelve pounds before lunch," Al said. "Are you sure this is your first day, son?" And Patrick smiled. When he wrote the number in the notebook next to my brother's name, his fingers rubbed together, dry as paper.

He turned to me. "Your turn, Melissa." I lifted my

bucket, smiling at the name. "Six pounds," he said, squinting at the needle. He made a neat number six next to M-e-l-i-s-s-a, then pulled a big pitcher and poured bright red liquid into two white paper cups.

"It's Kool-Aid," he said, handing us each a cup. "Cherry. Worst thing that can happen to you out here is dehydration. That's when you start to see little men marching on the ground. So help yourself to water, if you didn't bring your own." He motioned to a large water jug at the end of the counter.

The Kool-Aid was icy cold and tangy-sweet and I finished it in one grateful gulp. Al said, "Most kids eat lunch over there, in the shade of that big chestnut tree. If you sit too close to the hedge, you'll get prickles."

"Where are they?" I asked him. "The other kids?"

He shrugged. "I don't know what they're doing half the time. Everything is different now. Not like the old days. But you'll see them around."

While I asked Al about the bathroom, Patrick grabbed our lunches and started for the shady spot underneath the tree. Al pointed to a dirt path at the far edge of the field. "Follow that around the curve. There's an outhouse at the end. Watch out for bears."

"Really?"

He winked. "A person should always watch out for bears."

When I caught up with Patrick, he was already on the ground, his back against the tree trunk, chewing on his sandwich. Berry picking had given him an appetite, something new for my skinny brother. I stood over him. "I have to go to the bathroom."

"Okay."

"You don't want to come?"

He shook his head.

"There might be bears." I waited a moment, hoping that might change his mind, like he'd either want to see a bear or protect me from one. But he didn't, so I turned and followed the narrow path of beaten-down grass, up and around the corner. At the far end of the path I saw what looked like an old wooden coffin tipped up on its end.

The door creaked open on rusted hinges. When I stepped inside, I almost choked. The toilet seat was a hole cut out of a plank of wood, balanced over another hole dug straight into the ground. Fat black flies buzzed in crazy circles around the hole, guarding their treasure. An ancient roll of toilet paper balanced on a nail stuck in the wall. I looked up. Instead of a ceiling, there was just a square space of clear blue sky.

I'd never seen an outhouse like that before—only those sweet-smelling plastic kind that you see at fairs and construction sites. And I wouldn't say I liked it, exactly. But it was real. Like everything else in the blueberry field, it was real.

I got out quick and ran back up the path to the tree. I did my best to describe the outhouse to Patrick, the crazy flies, the patch of sky overhead, the seat that was a plank of wood, and the hole dug straight into the ground. I said, "I wonder what happens when the hole gets full?"

He laughed and I laughed. Our hands were stained and dirty and looked like strangers' hands against the pure whiteness of our bread, but it didn't bother us. We ate our sandwiches and stared at each other in amazement: *the best food we'd ever eaten!*

Bugs marched through grasses and scuttled in the dirt, keeping the earth alive. Had they always been there, those bugs? How had I not seen that the world was in motion, every inch of it, every moment? I leaned back and through the thin fabric of my T-shirt felt the rough bark of the tree. I crunched an apple down to the core, and wondered about the farmer who had grown it.

"This came from an actual tree, Patrick," I said suddenly, holding up my apple core. "Someone picked it. Like we are picking blueberries."

Patrick snorted. "Of course, Missy. Of course."

But what I was really trying to say was this: Your

dinner comes from a grocery store and then—*WHAM*—it doesn't. It comes from dew and dirt and sunshine. From old man hands and clanging metal buckets. It comes from flies and heat and voices without faces.

It comes from me. Melissa.

CHAPTER 9

AFTER LUNCH, MY FINGERS SLOWED DOWN, BUT MY mind raced with crowding thoughts: *This is too hot; I'm going to be sick; I might even die.* Sweat rolled down my neck, trickled past my collar and all the way down my back. I said out loud, "This is pure misery, Patrick. Pure, pure misery."

"What do you want me to do about it?"

"Don't you think it's time to go?"

"What does the sun tell you?"

I knew he was teasing, but I squinted up anyway. "It's two o'clock," I said, surprised at how the sky-clock made perfect sense. "I'm pretty sure. Let's go."

Patrick said, "I want to fill this bucket first." I could

tell by his voice he was doing the math on forty-two cents and all his pounds, planning out his back-to-school jeans and high-top sneakers shopping trip. "I'll meet you there."

Walking back through the row, I stopped to pick a handful of berries. I looked for the most perfectly blue and plump and firm ones, the ones that seemed to jump into my hand. I dropped them gently into the pocket of my T-shirt. At the weigh station, Al poured my big bucket into a flat wooden crate and smoothed them with his giant hand. "You pick nice berries, Melissa," he said. "You and your brother are good hard workers with no shenanigans."

Shenanigans. I said the word to myself, over and over, and decided to use it every chance I got. Al added up my pounds and wrote the number on a slip of paper. "Take this up to the office. Bev will give you your money."

As I walked up the tire-track road, the giant hedge cast a dark shadow, reminding me of the second farm on the other side. I stared at my feet and the small cloud of dust they kicked up. From the golden grass at the edge of the road, brown grasshoppers popped like crazy springs when I stepped too near their hiding spots, startling me every time.

The window underneath the OFFICE sign was closed. I

knocked lightly and waited. When I'd waited and knocked again and got no answer, I crossed the gravel drive and sat where the giant hedge threw down a small patch of shade in the scraggly weeds.

As I sat and waited, a long line of black ants marched in front of my feet. Their line stretched out all the way down the drive and then curved into the hedge and disappeared. Where were they going?

I tried to imagine what it looked like on the other side of the hedge. Was it an exact mirror image? Or a dark and twisted land? The prickles from the hedge scratched at my back, and I got the creepy kind of shivers. I scrambled to my feet and ran back across the drive to the office window. I knocked again, this time for real. *Bang, bang, bang.*

"Hold your horses!" came a shout from behind the closed door. A moment later the door opened and a woman stepped out. Before she closed it again I caught a glimpse of the kitchen behind her, and I even smelled something cooking.

She settled herself into a tall chair and, with a yank of her arm, opened the window all the way. She leaned forward and squinted right into my face. "What's the matter? You looked spooked."

"What? No—"

"You want your money?"

"Yes, okay." I dug the slip of paper out of my pocket. "Al said I—"

The woman reached out and took the paper. "Most kids wait until three o'clock. That's the official quitting time. We don't like them hanging around up here, getting into berry fights or dumping gravel down each other's pants."

"Oh," I said. "Sorry. Al didn't tell me."

She smiled then, and everything about her face softened. "Well, you must be the type of kid who wouldn't do that." She pulled out a clipboard and asked for my name.

I started to say Missy, but remembered Melissa just in time. She scanned the list and then frowned. "Funny, I don't see you."

"My mom, this morning. She probably told you my name was Missy. But I mostly go by Melissa."

She nodded. "Missy McKenzie. I see you right here. Now I remember. You have a brother, too. Your mom is a nice woman." I watched her cross off Missy and write Melissa. Next to it she wrote thirteen pounds.

"She said you were nice, too."

Bev sighed. "I'm nice first thing in the morning, when I have a cup of coffee in my hand. Right about now, though, I'm not so nice."

I glanced down at her hands, counting out bills and change from a metal box. Next to the box was a paperback book, with a woman and a castle on the cover. The woman wore a red cape, and her tumbling dark hair reached the middle of her back. "You like to read?" Bev asked. "You want a soda? I don't usually offer, but—"

"No, thanks," I said to soda, even though I wanted it so badly my throat tightened at the thought. "And I do like to read. I like adventure stories. And fantasy."

"Oh, those. I guess I liked those as a kid. Now I like romance. Do you like romance?"

"Not really," I said. "I've seen enough romance."

She tipped back her head and laughed with her mouth so wide open I could see all the way down her throat. It scared me right then, thinking of the inside of bodies. It scared me thinking that the inside of all our throats looked more or less the same.

"You've seen enough romance, huh?" She chuckled as she pushed the money across the counter. "There you go, hon. It might not seem like much today, but put it in a jar and count it on Friday. It adds up."

I tucked the bills and change, five dollars and forty-six cents, into my pocket and said good-bye to the lady named Bev. I looked up at the sun, reminding myself that, next time, I would wait until three o'clock. From my tiny patch of shade near the prickly hedge, I sat and stared down the tire-track road. Finally, I saw them, small groups of kids, trudging up the hill, trailing sweatshirts in the dirt. I thought: *These are the faces behind the voices.* And I wanted to hide.

But I stayed still and kept watch for Patrick. Cars pulled in, one right after the next, and kids peeled away from their groups to pile into various backseats. When our own car turned into the lot, I jumped up and dashed over. First thing Mom said was, "Where's your brother?"

I threw my extra clothes on the floor and crawled in next to Claude's car seat. "He's coming. Any minute." I wiggled my purple fingers at my sticky-damp brother, making him laugh so hard he got the hiccups.

"You two were supposed to stick together out there."

"We did." Hot vinyl stuck to the back of my bare legs. When I lifted them off the seat they made a sucking sound. "Mom, it's so hot back here!"

"What do you want me to do about it, Missy?" My mother tapped her fingers impatiently.

Panting like a dying cat I asked, "Can't you turn on the air-conditioning?"

"It's broken, Missy. Roll down the window."

I watched over Claude's round, hiccupping head until I finally saw Patrick, his skinny shoulders and slight limp, making his way up the hill. "There he is, Mom. There's Patrick."

"Pat-ick!" Claude shouted, and Patrick glanced over, grinned, and waved.

I watched him step up to the office window and hand his slip to Bev. I watched him shove the money deep into the pocket of his shorts. As he settled in the front seat of the car, Mom glanced at his stained fingers and flushed cheeks. "Well?" she asked. "How was it?"

"Great!" He turned and said to me, "Twenty-two pounds, Missy."

"Wow," I said. "You might win the prize."

"Go!" Claude shouted, and we all laughed.

The breeze, when it filled the car, brought with it the smell of pine needles and honeysuckle, summer grass and fresh dirt. It had always been there, the breeze, but that was the day I understood it carried scent, and that scent was made up of countless ingredients, some I could recognize and some I could not.

I felt the back of my T-shirt, soaked with sweat, and looked at Patrick's neck, pink from the sun and covered with a thin layer of dirt. I reached into my T-shirt pocket and carefully cupped the small handful of perfect blueberries I'd saved for this moment. I held one up to Claude, who opened his mouth and let me plop it in, just like a baby bird.

CHAPTER 10

THE NEXT MORNING PATRICK WAS AT THE KITCHEN counter making sandwiches and I was across from him eating cereal when Mom walked in, holding Claude, who was droopy from being pulled out of his warm bed. She shook her head. "I don't know about this."

I stopped chewing. Hadn't she noticed Patrick making our lunches, without being asked? Quickly, I put my cereal bowl in the sink and eased Claude from my mother's arms. I found his sweater and buttoned it over his kitty pajamas. "I dreamy cats," he said. His sleepy eyes moved from one corner of the kitchen to the other, trying to figure out where they all had gone.

Patrick finished making our lunches and then gulped

down the smelly protein drink that was supposed to give him muscles. While Mr. Coffee spit out its last drops, I shifted Claude to my hip and pulled Mom's favorite mug from the cupboard. I filled it with dark, steaming coffee and stirred in a tablespoon of cream, just the way she liked it.

She smiled when I handed it to her. "Thanks, honey."

In the backseat of the car, I read Claude his favorite picture book and even did all the voices. When I was done he said, "More boo-berries?"

"Yes," I said. "I'll bring you more blueberries today."

I glanced at my mother's face in the rearview mirror, hoping she would hear how nice I was being and how happy Claude sounded. I could only see her eyes and forehead, but that was enough to know that she looked tired.

I felt myself getting light-headed—a feeling I had a lot right after Dad first moved out of the house. It was the feeling that I was about to lose something big and important, that my life was about to spin away, and that I'd be left swirling somewhere, either high into the air or down a deep drain.

When the car turned onto the country road, I leaned my head against the window to study the same horses, the same cows, and the same weathered houses squatting in their damp brown fields. I didn't want this to be the last time I'd see them.

"We're closer to the water here," Mom said suddenly. "You can feel it in the air. It's just . . . thick."

She let out a sigh, like she was thinking of something all her own. It made me remember that she had been a person, long before she had become my mother. She had been a person with thoughts and feelings that didn't have anything to do with me. How strange.

Al looked happy when we ran up to his cart, flushed and breathless. "Where's your sweatshirt, Melissa?" He handed me my two buckets and penciled M-e-l-i-s-s-a in his notebook.

"I got so hot yesterday," I said. My only extra layer was a long-sleeved T-shirt, leaving my bare legs covered in goose bumps.

Al said, "It'll warm up soon. Let's put you back on row thirty-six. You're probably almost done with it, aren't you?"

Patrick and I answered at the exact same time. Only I said *no* while he said *yes*.

Al narrowed his eyes and looked from Patrick to me. "You know," he started, "a lot of kids don't like to stay on the same bush, or even the same row. They jump from bush to bush, looking for the best berries. Bush Hopper. Row Hopper. The trouble with being a hopper is you never settle down and see what's right in front of you. You're not being fair to the bush, the row, or yourself. Stick to a bush until you've picked all the berries. Don't skip it because the one next to it looks more promising. I'll tell you something. The berries down the row are just the same as the ones in front of your face. And this is not just about berry picking, either. This is about life."

It was like in a movie—the part near the end where the old guy delivers the line that makes everyone stand perfectly still or clasp hands or turn to one another and hug and laugh and cry. I said, "Okay, Al. Okay." And I meant it.

But back on the tire-track road Patrick snorted. "I didn't know blueberries were a religion."

I punched him on the shoulder. "Hey, think of it as camp, remember? Constance and Allie say they always teach you that kind of stuff at camp."

We reached the wooden marker with the faded 36. I took one side—same side as before—and Patrick took the other. The field was quiet, wrapped in its heavy fog and damp chill. Taking in a deep breath, I began to recognize the smell that came with morning—clean and sharp and sweet. It was the smell of early morning dirt, still wet with dew, and later I would notice how it changed into something different, something soft and rich and smooth with the warmth of the sun.

And that's when the voices would come out, too, with the sun. Another secret of the blueberry fields.

CHAPTER 11

I WAS ALL-THE-WAY BURNING HOT BEFORE I EVEN
noticed that the sun had turned to high. Also, the voices
were out, and I wondered how long they'd been shouting.
I shaded my eyes to check the sun, just shy of its noon
position. "Patrick," I said, "time for lunch."

At the weigh station, Al set our buckets on the old
metal scale and wrote numbers next to our names. When
he handed us our paper cup of cherry Kool-Aid, my throat
tingled even before I drank it. With lunch bags in hand,
Patrick led the way to the same shady spot underneath
the giant tree.

"Don't you have to go to the bathroom?" I asked my
brother.

He shook his head, already biting into his sandwich.

Once again I followed the narrow footpath. A pencil-thin garter snake cut a quick line next to my feet, and I watched until it slid into the dry grass and disappeared. At the remote edge of the field was the little wooden coffin outhouse, standing on its end. I was in and out in less than a minute, before the flies had time to settle on me. It wasn't so bad, really. Our toilets at home with flushing water, now maybe that was the strange thing.

That's what I was thinking as I walked back along the narrow path, feeling the sun on the top of my head. The idea of pipes and tubes, underground sewers connecting us all in ways I'd never thought about, was so new to me, so enormous and unexpected, that I didn't notice what had changed until I got close to the tree. My brother was still there, just as I'd left him. But there was someone else underneath that tree, too.

It was a girl.

And just her standing there made the world look different.

I walked up slowly. The girl stood looking down at Patrick, and they were both laughing. Patrick stopped when I reached them.

"This must be your sister," the girl said. "You must be Missy." Her sneakers were white and her shorts were white. She held a shiny silver lunch box.

"Melissa." I settled in next to my brother.

"I'm Shauna," she said, plopping down in front of us and making a tight little triangle. Patrick nearly choked out his carrot.

The girl named Shauna shook back her shiny black hair and smiled straight at me, crinkling up her eyes. She wore a purple bikini top with straps so thin, they could have been used as dental floss. "Patrick said this is your second day. It's terrible, isn't it?"

I pulled my sandwich from its plastic bag and glanced down at my hands, grubby against the white bread. I suddenly wished there was a place to wash them. "Why are you here, then?" I asked. "If it's so terrible?"

"Punishment. Pure punishment." She opened her lunch box and took out a water bottle wrapped in tinfoil. "Keeps it cold," she explained. She unscrewed the lid and took a tiny sip. Then she licked her lips and said, "Aren't you going to ask why I'm being punished?"

"Yes," stammered Patrick. "Why? For what?"

I looked at him in surprise. His face was red and he'd stopped chewing. "What's the matter with you?" I demanded. But he was staring at Shauna with his mouth half open.

Shauna said, "I borrowed some money from my

mother's wallet. I was going to pay it back, but she called it stealing. This is to teach me the value of money."

"Oh," said Patrick.

"I was originally supposed to go to tennis camp in California," she added. "But my mom went rabid and canceled it. Well, of course she changed her mind back again, but by then my spot was gone. So she looked around until she found the absolute worst place to dump me. And here I am. Don't you have hand wipes?"

"What?" Patrick asked, dazed.

"No," I said. I took another bite of my sandwich. "We don't." I noticed her shoes, which were spotless, like she'd been walking on brand-new carpet all day.

"Here." She held out two packs of premoistened antibacterial hand wipes. "I have a million."

"No thanks," I said. "Our mother doesn't believe in antibacterial."

Patrick took the wipe. After he cleaned his hands he uncrossed his scrawny legs, and then crossed them again. He cleared his throat as if to speak, but only a weird squeak came out.

"What?" I said to him. "Spit it out."

"You're the first person we've met," Patrick finally managed. He cleared his throat again. "The first other kid I mean. We hear them but we don't see them."

"Oh, they'll be out. We were here a few days before the rain started, so we've already learned some things."

"Like what?" I asked.

"Well, the longer you wait for lunch, the easier the afternoon will be. The afternoons are torture. Absolute torture." She fanned her hand over her face.

"You didn't wait," I said. "For lunch."

"Oh, most of my day is lunch, actually," she laughed. Patrick laughed, too. I didn't laugh. I never laugh just because other people do. It's one of my absolute biggest pet peeves. If I could start a club it would be the Don't Laugh Unless Something Is Really Funny Club.

I thought about how we had to beg our mom and dad to let us come. "You don't think they want to be out here? The other kids?"

"Of course not. We all want to be at the lake. Don't you want to be at the lake?" She glanced across to Al's weigh station. Then she lowered her voice. "You know, though, you can actually have some fun out here. I'll introduce you to the other campers. You'll see."

"We should get to work, Patrick," I said. The idea of other kids made me nervous. I liked things the way they were, with just my brother.

Patrick acted like he hadn't heard me. "How many pounds have you picked?" His voice was low and strange, like he was trying out for a part in the school play.

"Three. Or something. Nearly one of those little buckets. Just enough to get my Kool-Aid." She smiled and leaned forward, close enough so we could smell her hair—sweet and clean, like fresh green apples. "I can't imagine a worse place than this, but if I got kicked out, I'm sure my mom would find one."

Patrick laughed and nodded his stupid bobblehead. "Yeah, mine too."

I glared at him. Traitor. Liar. I scrambled to my feet and brushed the dust off my shorts. I was hoping some of it would find its way to Shauna's smooth, bare belly or land in that silky, sweet-apple hair. "Come on. We have berries to pick, Patrick. No time for shenanigans."

"Hold on a sec—"

"Let's *go*, Patrick. Mom said we had to stick together."

Shauna looked at my brother and laughed. "That's okay. Go ahead. But at least tell me what row you're on."

"Thirty-six." He got to his feet and smiled down at her with a look that was both shy and grateful.

She smiled back, straight into his eyes. "Maybe I'll come and find you," she said. "Just don't yell 'Row Hopper' if you see me coming through the bushes."

"I won't," Patrick said. Hypnotized monkey. "I never would."

"I might," I said as I walked away.

Shauna called, "Good-bye, Patrick. Good-bye, Melissa." And hearing her say my fake name like that made me melt—for a moment, anyway—just like my brother had.

I spent the rest of the afternoon listening for the rustle of branches, the clanging of buckets, or the shuffle of approaching footsteps, but Shauna didn't find her way to row thirty-six. When the sun got close to its three o'clock mark I said, "Okay, Patrick. Let's go."

My brother sighed and I knew that he, too, had been waiting for Shauna to appear. And even though she hadn't, just the thought of her filled our space with something else, something new, something other than the two of us out there.

"Maybe we'll see Shauna," he said finally. And I could tell he was looking for an excuse to say her name.

CHAPTER 12

SHAUNA SHOWED UP EARLY THE NEXT DAY, BEFORE the sun had the chance to dry off the leaves. I heard a crashing through the bushes and thought, "Bear!" But before I could shout out a warning, I saw the flash of a white tennis shoe and then I knew.

She squeezed through to my row, wearing a different colored bikini top, white with yellow stripes. Goose bumps and drops of dew dotted her bare stomach.

"Ta-da!" she said.

I glared. "What's that supposed to mean?"

"It means I found you." She looked past me and then crouched down to see the other side of the row. "Where's your brother?"

"Not here," I said quickly, which wasn't a complete lie. He wasn't exactly where we were standing, so he wasn't technically "here." Anyway, it didn't work. Patrick must have had extrasensory girl perception, or else the green-apple shampoo scent was seriously that strong, because before I even heard the branches move, Patrick was on my side of the row, looking more stupid than ever.

"Hey," he said, smiling in this weird shy way.

"Hey," she said, smiling back. "So you're still here—on the same row?"

"Well, yeah." His face was red, and he stood like he was flexing his chest or something. I snorted.

She said, "The best berries are on the other side of the field. I don't know why the old guy stuck you two out here."

"His name is Al," I said. "Where did he *stick* you?" There were words underneath my words, and Patrick glanced at me with a warning in his eyes. But Shauna didn't seem to notice.

"Just a few rows away," she said. "But I don't stay there."

Just then I realized that something was missing from her outfit—something besides a shirt. "You don't have a bucket," I said. "You don't have a picking bucket."

She shrugged. "Whatever. I hate those things. They get my shorts dirty. Come with me, Patrick. I'll show you where the really good berries are. You, too, Melissa."

She was including me *and* using my fake name. I tried to hold on to my hate.

"Come on, guys," she said softly. "I'll show you around."

Patrick made a clumsy move toward his big bucket, but he almost tripped because his eyes were stuck to her yellow-and-white stripes.

I said quickly, "No. We stay here. We're supposed to stay here. It's our job."

"Then you stay here, Missy," Patrick said firmly. He picked up his big bucket. "I'm going."

I felt blood rush to my head: dizzy. The words were out before I knew they would be, before I realized the threat that they were. "Then I hope you enjoy your last day."

Patrick froze. "What? What are you talking about?"

I took a deep breath, so my voice would sound stronger than I actually felt. "Mom said to stick together out here. And if she finds out that you ditched me—"

"I didn't ditch you."

"You're about to."

"Because you're making the choice to stay here—"

"It's not a choice, Patrick. It's the *rule*."

Patrick stared at me, and what I saw in his eyes made me look down at my shoes.

Shauna said, "Well—"

"Don't go," Patrick told her. He turned back to me. "Missy—"

I started picking again, even though I could hardly see the bush in front of me.

Shauna said softly, "If you ever want to find me, Patrick, listen for the radio. I'm always around a radio. Just follow the sound."

"Okay," he said. "I'll find you."

I cleared my throat loudly.

"Shut up, Missy."

"It's Melissa," I said.

"Good-bye, Melissa," Shauna said. "Catch you later, Patrick." And then she was gone. And my brother might as well have been gone, too.

Later, when the radio turned on somewhere in the middle of the field, I heard him catch his breath. But other than that, the only sounds were the rustle of bushes, the soft tumble of berries, and the bugs and bees, making their own kind of music.

The thing is, I'd always had Patrick. When Mom and Dad split, Patrick and I traveled back and forth together, just the two of us. It was too confusing for Claude, or too hard for Mom, I don't know which. So back and forth, from house to house, just me and Patrick. We stayed the same. He was the one person I could count on.

Both Mom and Dad always said the right things, all the things they were supposed to say. *This isn't about you, it's about us. We'll always be your parents together, even though we're not living together. You kids don't ever have to take sides.*

But the truth was: They had no idea. If I wasn't on a side, I'd be lost in the middle. Without a side, I wouldn't be anywhere at all. So I did take a side. Patrick was my side. He had to be. And I'd do anything to keep him there, even if it made him hate me. That would only be temporary. After a while, things would get back to the way they were. They had to. Otherwise, I wouldn't have anyone. I wouldn't have a side.

When the sun pointed to noon I announced, "Time for lunch, Patrick," like nothing was wrong. He came without speaking. I said, "Are you ever going to talk to me again?"

He stared straight ahead, and I could see how his jaw was clenched tight.

"You look like Dad," I told him.

"Shut up," he said finally, through that clenched jaw. And we walked the rest of the way with *shut up* echoing between us.

We ate underneath the tree, but the world had gone

as flat and dry as my sandwich. On the walk back to our row, a truck rumbled down the tire-track road, the bright orange truck from up at the house. As we stepped into the tall grass to let it pass, I squinted to get a glimpse of the driver. I saw a bright green cap and not much more.

"That must be Moose," I said, but Patrick had already slipped back into our row.

I stood where I was, though, determined to see what a farmer named Moose looked like.

The truck bounced to the end of the road. It came to a squeaky stop in front of Al's weigh station, then the bright orange door swung open.

Here's the thing: with a name like Moose you expect someone big, like a guy who plays professional football or makes his living carrying refrigerators on his back. But this Moose wasn't a moose. He was the opposite of moose. From where I stood I couldn't be sure, but he looked even smaller than me. And seeing that, even from a distance, gave my stomach a funny sort of tingle.

I waited and watched as he loaded up the crates of berries from Al's stack. When he climbed back into the truck, I dashed to my row and slipped between the first bushes. "Patrick," I called, running up the row. "Patrick—I saw Moose! I saw—" but then I stopped, out of breath. I stopped because I saw four feet where there should have been two. And they were facing each other. Four feet!

"Hey!" I said. "I see you there. I see exactly what you're doing there!" As I pushed through to the other side, the feet moved apart.

"Hello, Melissa," Shauna said sweetly.

Without a word, I turned and squeezed back through the bushes, to my side. Because that's when I understood: There's no stopping certain things.

CHAPTER 13

"YOU ACT STUPID AROUND HER."

"No, I don't."

"Yes. You do." He was supposed to say, "No, I don't" again. But he didn't.

It was late Friday afternoon, and we had officially completed our first week of blueberry picking. We were packed, freshly showered, and waiting for Dad to pick us up for the weekend. Mom had taken Claude to the park, which she often did on Friday afternoons so he wouldn't be confused by Dad's coming and going without him. As directed by the Parenting Plan, Dad got Claude every Monday and Wednesday evening, and also got to see him on most weekends, but not yet to spend the night. Mom had this thing that Claude was too young to be away from her overnight. I knew it was something they fought about, but never in front of us.

I put on my 3-D glasses and stared across the living room at the paint samples, still taped to the wall. They looked like long yellow bandages. I said, "I wonder if Mom is ever going to paint this room."

"When are you going to stop wearing those stupid glasses, Missy?"

I shrugged. "Maybe I'll start wearing them in the blueberry field. What do you think Shauna would say about that?"

"Why don't you like her, Missy? She's nice to you."

I thought of her bright bikini tops and her shiny black hair. "Because—" but I stopped. I didn't exactly know how to answer that question.

Patrick said, "You just want everything to stay the same forever."

"That's not true." Still, his words made me feel a deep tug in my stomach, the way truth can sometimes do.

I turned away and looked up at the clock. Nearly five. I heard the car in the drive and grabbed my weekend bag. "Come on, Patrick," I said. "Time for our second life."

That weekend was, at first, like any other. We watched TV, ate dinner, played Monopoly, and went to bed. As usual. In the morning we got up late, ate strawberry pancakes, and watched more TV. As usual. Everything was like usual until Sunday. Sunday lunch. And even Sunday lunch was as usual.

And then it happened, right after lunch, when the sun was filling the kitchen with a warm, yellow glow. Dad was at the freezer, pulling out two boxes of frozen treats. Tessa, sitting across from us, smiled way too much. She said, "So, how's the blueberry business?"

I ignored her, like I always did, while Patrick smiled and nodded his head. "It's good. Really good," he said.

I made a loud cough—the kind that sounds like you might throw up. Tessa jumped in her seat, but Patrick pretended not to hear. "Are you okay, Missy?" Tessa asked.

I made the sound again, and this time rolled my eyes and let my tongue hang out of my mouth. She turned away quickly. "You're both so tan," she said, looking only at Patrick.

Patrick yanked up his T-shirt sleeve. "It gets super hot in the afternoon," he said, pointing out how pale his shoulders were compared to his arms.

I gagged again. I was just about to say something about bikinis, when Dad set the ice-cream boxes on the table. "Kids," he said loudly, "we have some news."

My heart did one big thump and I sat up quickly. My foot, finding Patrick's underneath the table, pressed hard against it. When his foot pressed back, I knew we were thinking the same thing: Dad was using different words, but the funny strain in his voice was exactly the same as when he'd told us he'd be moving out. Suddenly, the only thing I had was Patrick's foot. Nothing else mattered.

I pulled the 3-D glasses from my pocket and adjusted them on my face. That extra border around my eyes gave me a comforting distance from my dad and Tessa and the flowers in the middle of the table. I pressed my Spectacular Vision Button and said in a robot voice, "You—are—breaking—up—that—is—your—news."

For once, Patrick didn't snort or make me feel stupid. His foot pressed harder into mine, not in a mean way, but in a "hold on tight" way. I pressed back, just the same.

"No, Missy," Dad said gently. "We're getting married."

I looked around the kitchen with its restored wood cupboards and antique-store knobs and tried to swallow the ache that was rising in my chest.

From somewhere far off, I heard Patrick let out a long, shaky breath. I felt his foot slip away. It hadn't occurred to me until that moment that Patrick might have been guarding the same small dream I had been: As long as

Dad and Tessa weren't married, there was still a chance for him and Mom to get back together. Now, three small words changed all that. I thought nothing would ever feel as bad as Dad moving out of our house.

I was wrong.

After what seemed like a long time, Dad pushed the boxes of frozen treats over to us. I said, "Just what we need—frozen crap on a stick."

"Missy!" Dad's voice was stern.

"Missy," Tessa interrupted softly. "I have a question for you. A big favor."

I didn't look at her. Pretended not to hear.

"Missy, I'd like you to be my maid of honor. If you would."

I froze. Words swirled around in my head, but none would go together in any sort of order. They were all like mismatched magnets that, instead of clicking together, pushed away at one another with all their might.

Out of the corner of my eye I saw Tessa's hand, like a sidestepping crab, moving across the table toward my own. I reached out and grabbed a frozen treat from one of the boxes, busying my hands with the wrapper.

"Hmm," I said, "my favorite." And it actually was my favorite—just a plain vanilla ice-cream sandwich. I watched with relief as Tessa's crab hand slid back to her side of the table. *Ha!* I wanted to say. *Just because you're marrying my dad does not mean you can ever, ever, ever touch me like a mother would.*

"Missy," Dad said quietly, "Tessa asked you a question."

Question? Like there was a question?

"Well, thanks for asking," I said, cramming my mouth so full of chocolate wafer and vanilla ice cream that I was sure no one, not even Patrick, could understand me. "But I think I'm busy that day."

As I met their confused stares, I suddenly felt so clever and funny that I started to laugh. Maybe when you get to be a grown-up you know all the different laughs a body can have, but this particular laugh took me completely by surprise. It was powerful, uncontrollable, and came straight from the bottom of my belly. My belly, in fact, was shaking, and so were my shoulders. This was a laugh that took over my body—made my eyes sting with tears and my throat tighten. The ice cream and wafer got stuck in my throat, actually seemed to harden into a tiny lump in my throat, and I started to gag.

"She's choking!" I heard Patrick cry out. "Do something, Dad!"

And the next thing I knew Dad was pounding me on the back and Tessa was punching me in the stomach and my body was trying to throw up and breathe and cry, but it couldn't do any of those things, and the whole time Patrick's voice chanted crazily in my ears, "She's choking, she's choking. Dad, Dad, Dad. She's choking."

And then, in an instant, everything stopped. The back pounding from Dad, the stomach punching from Tessa, the belly heaving from me.

My 3-D glasses were hanging by one ear and I slowly tucked them back on the other ear, like maybe they'd actually help me see what was there, right in front of me on the table.

Even as I stared at it for several seconds, I could not make sense of what I was looking at. Because mixed with the gooey mound of ice cream and chocolate wafer cookie was something else. Was this from my body? Had I coughed up an internal organ? And, if so, what organ could it be? Had I choked up my heart? Did this whole Dad/Mom/Tessa thing cause me to choke up my very own heart?

That seemed to be the most logical conclusion except for the fact that I was still sitting at the table, breathing, which meant my heart must be in there somewhere, beating. And also for the fact that this thing, in the middle of the ice-cream mess, looked a lot like a ball. A bright, round ball. And although that might have explained several things about me, I didn't think it would be possible for anyone to live to the age of twelve with a ball for a heart.

"*Dad,*" I heard myself whisper. I wanted to see his face. "How did a ball get inside me?" I wondered if maybe I'd swallowed one as a baby. I couldn't shake the thought that all my organs were brightly colored and perfectly round.

Dad grabbed the box of frozen treats off the table. "It's the gumball inside," he sputtered out finally.

What? What was he saying? I must have eaten at least two thousand of these things in my lifetime and never once was there a gumball inside. *A gumball inside the ice cream?*

"It's new, Missy! I told you. It's a new product. We're testing it."

Patrick took the box from Dad's hand. "New," he said, pointing to the words in red letters. "Gumball Surprise Inside Each Treat!"

I stared at the words. Even in Spectacular 3-D, they didn't make sense. "But this is an ice-cream sandwich. Who wants gum inside their ice-cream sandwich?" I grabbed the box and examined it closely. "Choking hazard—it says right here!"

"Keep reading," said Patrick. He tapped the small print with his finger.

"Not for children under three," I read.

"Exactly. Exactly." *Tap, tap.*

I looked at my dad. "So what? This is my fault?"

"No one is saying it's your fault, Missy."

"Whose fault?" I shouted at my dad. "Ice cream is now a choking hazard. That is someone's fault. *This is someone's fault!*"

I stood and stomped out of the kitchen, out of the house, certain that Patrick would follow me. But he didn't, which was sort of the worst thing about the whole miserable moment. Because all of a sudden, everything did seem like it was my fault. I had ruined their perfect day. I had left a big blob of choked-up mess right on their perfect kitchen table.

But how was a person to know? When someone changes the rules, they should say it out loud. Ice cream was now a choking hazard; it was spelled out right there on the box. But what if a person didn't know where to look? What if they didn't know they were *supposed* to look?

All the new rules in my life. I knew they were there, spelled out somewhere. I knew they were there because I could feel them, pressing at me from all around. I could see them in other people's eyes when they looked at me. I knew I wasn't doing things right. But where was a person supposed to look for them, these new rules?

Someone needed to tell me. Someone really needed to say them out loud.

CHAPTER 14

BACON. THE NEIGHBORHOOD REEKED OF IT. STANDING ON the porch and smelling bacon, I wondered how everything could look and smell so Sunday normal. How could the lawns look so perfectly green, and the sidewalks so nicely swept? Didn't everyone know the world had just exploded?

I removed my 3-D glasses and put them in my pocket. When the door opened behind me I didn't turn around. It could only be one of three people, or two of three people, or three of three people. And there was only one of those people I wanted to see.

"Patrick?" My eyes were closed I was hoping so badly.

"Hey, Missy."

I let out a breath and turned to my brother. He held out my backpack. "I packed it for you."

"Good. Because I'm not going back in there."

"Yeah, that's what I figured."

"What happened after I left?"

"Your ice cream melted all over the table."

"What else?"

"Nothing."

"Something had to happen."

"Dad got a headache."

"Good," I said. "I hope she gets one, too. I hope their heads pop off. How can he do this? He knows nothing about her."

"We've known her for over a year, Missy."

"Still. I think we should hire a private detective. To do a background check."

Patrick laughed at me. Then he said, "She bought a dress for you. For being in the wedding."

"But I'm not going to be in the wedding. She can't make me. What about you?"

He shrugged. "I guess I'm supposed to wear a tuxedo."

"That's not what I meant. What did you say to them?"

"Nothing."

I snorted. I wanted to ask him about the dress, but I didn't want to say the words out loud. Saying the words

would be admitting that this was real. But the more I
thought about Tessa actually buying me a dress, the more
I wanted to know. What color was it? Was it long or short?
Did it have any beads or jewels? Sleeves or straps?

"So," I said finally, when I couldn't stand it any
longer, "did you see it?"

"What?"

"The dress."

"It was in the hall closet," Patrick said. "I guess she was
going to surprise you. You know, take it out, and you guys
would be all 'Oh, it's so beautiful,' and 'Oh, I'm so excited.'"
He'd changed his voice to sound like ladies at a tea party or
something and I couldn't help it—I laughed. Then I imagined
the moment, how it could have been with hugs and excitement and the big reveal of the special dress. The touching
stepmother/stepdaughter moment Tessa had hoped for.

"I'm never going to like her. I'm never going to be
any sort of maid of anything at their stupid wedding. I'm
never—" I stopped.

"Never what?" Patrick asked.

But I didn't actually know how to finish the list of
things I was never going to do. There were way too many.

Instead, I pulled out my 3-D glasses again and tried
to slip into a different dimension. But for once, I couldn't
get them to work. I was stuck. Right where I was.

CHAPTER 15

THE WEDDING WAS TO BE AT THEIR HOUSE. THAT was the next piece of news we got from Dad. He didn't mention ice-cream sandwiches, gumballs, or my near-death experience, so I didn't either. What he did say, was that the wedding would be there, in the lovely backyard, right at the end of summer. "So we're going to be busy," he said. "There's a lot to do and very little time."

For a special treat they took us out to an early dinner at a crappy pizza place—the kind with a ball pit and games with plastic prizes. "Well," Dad said, watching me pick at the crust, "I guess your old dad can do nothing right, huh, Missy?"

"It's fine, Dad. I'm just not hungry."

"The pizza's great, Dad." Patrick tore into another slice of greasy pepperoni. "We love this place."

"I thought you liked the games here," Dad said, still looking at me. "I thought we'd have fun with the games."

"I guess I'm just not in the mood to hit plastic squirrels on the head."

"They're gophers," Patrick said.

"Oh, gosh! Then let me at them."

We left more than half the pizza on the table. When Dad asked Patrick if he wanted to take it home, he shook his head sadly. Even Patrick had his limits. He did, however, pick up a rubber mallet on the way out and limply swing it at a line of singing gophers. He missed every one.

I hated when Tessa drove home with us. It meant Dad dropped us off without coming in to play with Claude. It meant I wouldn't have that one happy moment of pretending we could be a family again. And now there was the extra problem of Dad and Tessa's Big News. Did Mom even know?

"Does Mom know we're coming home late?" I asked as we turned onto our street.

Dad nodded.

"Does she know you're not coming in?"

"I called her before dinner."

"Does she know about you and—"

"Of course, Missy," he said, stopping me before I could finish the question. "We talk about everything concerning you kids."

Minutes later, when Patrick and I walked through the front door, we found Claude wandering aimlessly in the living room, sobbing for Daddy. When I asked, "What's wrong, Mr. Claudio?" he marched up and slapped me on the leg.

Mom was in her bedroom, putting away folded clothes. Usually she sang while she did those kinds of chores, but right then she was silent.

"I'm sorry, Mom," I said. "I'm sorry Dad didn't come in."

While Claude stomped up and down the hallway, Mom turned to look at me. "Come here," she said finally. She held out her arms and I fell into them. She stroked my hair, just like when I was little, and it felt so good that I stood there, rocking in her arms and trying not to cry.

Later, after Claude was tucked in bed, Mom ordered a late-night pizza, something the three of us did once in a while for a special treat. When she had suggested it, we didn't have the heart to tell her we weren't hungry. And that we'd already had pizza for dinner.

Sitting on the couch together, Patrick handed Mom a cup of peppermint tea in her favorite mug—the one we gave her for Mother's Day, back before Claude even, when things were still normal. It was one of those with a photograph transferred on, so it has the two of us, me and Patrick, grinning underneath a banner with the words WE ♥ MOM!

As Mom drank her tea, I watched the smiling face of me tip up and down. "You knew we weren't getting back together," she said. "There was never a chance of that."

"There was a chance," I said, without thinking.

"There wasn't. You knew that, didn't you, Patrick?"

Patrick nodded and struggled to swallow. He coughed and his face turned red.

I wanted to crawl back into my mother's lap. I wanted her to stroke my head and tell me that this wouldn't always feel so bad, just like she said to Claude when he fell down and scraped the skin off his knee. But even if she did, would I believe her?

"Tell me something nice," Mom said suddenly. "Let's talk about something nice." She set down her mug and picked up a slice of pizza.

Patrick said, "Dad finished his kitchen cupboards. They look nice." Mom's smile froze, but only for a moment. "I'm sorry, Mom," Patrick said, immediately realizing what a stupid thing that was to say, especially sitting in a room with bad green carpet and yellow paint samples taped on the wall.

Usually on these special pizza nights we would stay up for hours, talking or watching an old cowboy movie or playing Yahtzee. But the news had taken just about everything out of us. We cleaned our dishes and went to bed. But first I did something I hadn't done in a long time: I went over, wrapped my arms around my mother's neck, and kissed her good night. "I think his kitchen looks weird," I whispered to her. "Too many fancy things."

Mom gave me a squeeze and looked straight into my eyes. "Some people like fancy things, honey, and your dad works hard on that house. You know, it's okay to like being there. It's okay to like her, too."

"I hate her."

"Missy, listen to me. This marriage—it's a good thing. I'm glad your dad is happy with someone new. And she's a very nice person."

I fixed my eyes on the mug on the coffee table, those two smiling children. I tried to remember life back then. Before the split. "We need to get you a new mug," I said. "One with Claude."

"Missy. I need you to listen to this. It's important."

I nodded. But inside something new was beginning to happen. I was suddenly alive and awake. The words that had been choked down earlier now turned into something else: something hard and cold and sharp.

"Missy—" Mom said again.

"I know, Mom. I know." I sat up straight. Because right then I did know. I knew what I would do. I would mess it all up. I didn't know how, but I would mess it all up, all their nice things. Their perfect house and perfect life and perfect wedding—I would make a big, ugly mess of it all.

That night, before I went to bed, I pulled out the clothes I would wear for the morning. But when I got underneath the covers, I couldn't fall asleep. Finally, I made myself imagine I was standing in the middle of a blueberry field, where nothing could ever go wrong.

And the next thing I knew, it was morning.

CHAPTER 16

ACTUALLY, ONE THING COULD GO WRONG.

Shauna showed up after lunch on Monday, and before lunch on Tuesday, and just as the sun had dried off the dew on Wednesday.

The two of them were ridiculous.

They came up with games like Toss the Blueberry into the Other Person's Mouth and How Long Can a Blueberry Stay in a Bellybutton While Doing the Hula. They whispered and they laughed together. I spied on them constantly and once, through the bottom of the bushes, saw their toes touching.

"What are you doing?" I yelled it, over and over, until their toes moved apart.

On Thursday before lunch, I pushed through the bushes and looked in Patrick's big bucket. It was empty. "Patrick! You haven't even filled up one little bucket yet?"

"So?" he said.

I went up to him and said right in his ear, "You'll never get those jeans you want. And those shoes."

"So?" he said again.

"So," I said loudly. "You'll look stupid in high school next year."

Shauna laughed. "I guarantee that your brother will not look stupid in high school. I was a freshman last year, so I know what I'm talking about."

Pretending she was invisible, I pushed back through to my own side of the row. But I continued to spy on them through the thick branches, watching like they were a TV show that I hated, but for some reason, couldn't turn away from.

Friday afternoon was hot even before lunch, and the radios in the field clicked on early. Shauna shouted, "Whooo! Turn it up!"

"Whooo to you, Shauna!" a boy's voice called back. "Come over here!"

"You come over here!"

"No!" I hissed it through the bushes. "Tell them no!"

"What row are you on?" the voices called out. "Tell us what row!"

"No!" I hissed again. "Please!"

The voices, they scared me. The times I saw other kids in the field, like at the weigh station or waiting for a ride by the office, they were silent. Or, if they spoke, it was in quiet voices, voices meant for hiding. But in the cover of the bushes, their voices changed. I could only imagine different kids attached to these voices. Big and unpredictable and full of awful shenanigans.

Shauna glanced down at me, slumped in the weeds: grubby little sister girl. I knew how I looked to them.

She called out, "Tell us a joke, Smith Brothers. Maybe if you're funny enough I'll tell you which row we're on." Then she whispered to me, *"Don't worry. I won't let them come over."* And for a moment, I was grateful.

The voice I recognized as Smith One yelled, "Okay. Hey, everybody! I just finished reading a great book called *Fifteen Yards to the Outhouse*. It's written by I. P. Freely." Patrick laughed.

I said, "I don't get it."

"Shhh," Shauna said. "Keep listening."

Another voice, Smith Two, shouted back, "Oh, yeah.

The sequel is good. It's called, *Will He Make It?* by Betty Won't."

"Get it?" Patrick said. "I PEE freely."

Shauna laughed and said, "Bet—he—won't. Get it, Melissa? It's a play on words."

It took me a moment but I finally got the joke. Will he make it to the outhouse? Bet he won't. I started to laugh, too.

Shauna crouched down. She smiled at me through the bottom of the bushes. "You're actually laughing. I thought there was something wrong with your larynx."

"So?" I said. I didn't want to ask her what a larynx was.

"So. The middle one, Smith Two, is super cute. Probably your age. Do you want to meet him?"

"Of course not. Why would I?"

"Because we're people, silly girl. People need other people. Even monkeys do. They've done experiments. It's so incredibly sad, the monkeys who are all alone. They start to eat their own hands."

"Those are raccoons that get caught in traps," I said. "And I do have people. I have my own people. And, if you've forgotten, we're out here to do a job. Right, Patrick?" I waited, hoping Patrick would say something, stick up for me, but he was silent.

Shauna shook her head. "Are you kidding? This is

our camp. Camp Blueberry. Moose G's Blueberry Camp for Troubled Teens—" she stopped and then added, "Preteens, too."

"Oh, goody," I said. "Where are the canoes? Where's the campfire?" Even to my own ears I sounded like a crabby old lady.

"You'd be surprised at the fun we can have out here."

"Like what? What's so fun?" I got a whiff of green apple shampoo and couldn't help it—I breathed in deeply.

Shauna bit her bottom lip, as though that would be enough to keep the words from spilling from her mouth. I saw her glance back, over her shoulder. Were she and Patrick sharing some kind of secret? Were their eyebrows tapping out some sort of Morse code message?

"You know the hedge?" she said finally.

"Uh, yeah. I'm not blind." I thought about the warning from the first day: *Stay on this side of the hedge.*

"It was planted because of the blood feud."

The two words together made me feel queasy. "I know the brothers don't get along," I said. "I know all that already. Bev told my mom on the first day."

"But do you want to hear more?" Shauna asked. "About Moose? And his brother, Lyle? About the giant hedge?"

"No," I said. But I did. And she kept talking anyway.

"There's a reason the fields were divided. My mom

told me. She said the brothers had this huge fight, years ago. The whole town heard about it."

"Was there *blood*?" I couldn't help it. I had to know.

Shauna laughed. "Blood feud just means the fight is between people in the same family. You know. They have the same blood."

"I know that," I said, relieved about the blood, but angry with myself for giving in to her story, even with an important question.

"So we're exploring," she went on. "We want to find out what the fight was all about. We're searching every inch of this place."

I thought about Moose, about the one time I'd seen him jumping out of his shiny orange truck. "I'm going in," I said. And then, because I couldn't help myself I added, "Before I vomit."

Hot leaves slapped against my face as I marched to the front of the row. Even with the temperature so high the air had shiny waves, Al held his red plastic thermos-top cup filled with steaming coffee.

"Always a pleasure to see you, Melissa," he said. He put down his cup and poured my berries into a flat wooden crate and smoothed them out with his giant hand. "Look—I don't have to pick out a bad one or even remove a stem when I have a bucket from you."

He marked my pounds in his book. "You know, most people are in such a rush to make an extra buck that they give me all sorts of garbage. Leaves and stems and twigs. I even had a fellow fill the bottom with dirt so the bucket would weigh more."

I shook my head. Imagine!

Al handed me my paper cup filled to the top with cherry Kool-Aid. I drank it quickly, because it was so good and cold and sweet. Then I wiped my mouth and blurted, "I just heard something. I heard there's a blood feud out here. And also, I'm still wondering about the prize."

A muscle in Al's neck twitched so that, even when his voice sounded normal, I knew things were not. "Hard work is its own reward," he said. "Didn't I mention that before?"

"Yeah, but I don't really know what it means."

"It means stop thinking about the prize."

"Oh," I said. "Okay."

He picked up his coffee. "Blood feud, eh?"

"It was just something I heard." I wished I could take it back. The way he was looking at me made me feel like I was the one full of shenanigans. And I knew I should stop, before I made things worse, but my mouth wouldn't listen to my brain's good *shut up, Missy,* advice.

"So I was just wondering, is there one for real? And if

so, why would there be one in the first place? And what is it exactly?"

Al handed me another Kool-Aid and I wondered if he'd forgotten the first. I drank it quickly, before he could remember and take it back. He bent down to look me in the eye. "Who is saying it? Who is so full of information?"

"I don't know," I said. "Nobody. Just voices."

"Remember this, Melissa." Al wagged his sausage finger in a wise-old-man way. "People like to tell stories. It's wired into the brain of the human animal, and is both a good thing and a bad thing. I believe I gave you a piece of advice your first day here. Do you remember it?"

"Pick clean, stay on our own row, don't get dehydrated—"

"Don't believe everything you hear."

"What?"

"Do you remember me saying that?"

I nodded.

"I'm telling you the truth here. It's the kind of advice that will last you your whole lifetime. And probably the most valuable thing I can offer you."

"Okay," I said.

I thought he was done, but as I was grabbing my empty bucket, he cleared his throat and I knew he had more to say, like my mom always does when she gets riled up about something. This time his voice was different, like what he was saying was extra real. And he said my name, too. It made me stop.

"I don't usually talk about this, Melissa," he said, "but you are a kid worthy of trust. So here it is: We have two brothers on either side of this giant hedge here. Two brothers who divided their father's field. They cut it right down the middle. Took a big, strong farm and weakened it. If you want to call that a blood feud, so be it." He raised his giant hands helplessly. "And I'm not saying another thing about another thing."

"Okay," I said. "Thank you, Al."

My head was spinning when I got back to my row. As soon as my fingers fell into their picking rhythm, though, I forgot some of that confusing talk. My head got back to normal and it was just me and the berries.

They were my own reward.

CHAPTER 17

HERE'S SOMETHING ELSE I'VE LEARNED FROM MOM'S old cowboy movies: When the bolt of lightning strikes, the bad guy is coming into town. When the sky rumbles and the horses flare their giant horse nostrils, get ready— big change is on the way. That next Monday, when I woke to gray skies and a chilly wind, I didn't think about the lightning bolts in a cowboy movie. If I would have, I might have been prepared.

The weekend at Dad's had been mostly full of them doing wedding stuff, like sampling different pieces of white cake and looking at paper samples for invitations and moving boulders around in the backyard. I still didn't know how I was going to ruin the wedding. I needed my two best friends to help me come up with ideas, but every time I started writing a letter to them, it came out sounding like a weird TV version of a stupid fairy tale and I crumpled it up.

It didn't help that I'd gotten my first letter from them. The blue-lined pieces of paper could barely contain all their stories of canoe rides, backflips off the diving board, bow-and-arrow practice at the archery range, midnight hikes, a dead rattlesnake, campfires with skits and s'mores, and this one boy who was so cute, they'd practically forgotten about BM ("But don't forget to write in the book, if you see him!").

I was happy for my friends. I guess I was. I was supposed to be. But the truth was, maybe I wasn't. Maybe I felt the same way about them as I felt about Patrick.

Patrick had gone to the mall that weekend, to spend some of his blueberry money on a new swimsuit for going to the lake. The lake was where Shauna said he could find her when she wasn't in the blueberry field. When he came back from the mall with his new suit, he locked himself in the bathroom for an hour. And he never ended up going to the lake, after all.

So on Monday, bundled up in the backseat with Claude, I stared out the window at the horses with their heads hanging low in their chill, damp fields and said,

"Too bad you spent all your money on that fancy swimsuit you won't even use."

Mom squinted up at the sky. "It might clear up today. If it doesn't, it will soon. You'll get to the lake, Patrick."

Patrick didn't even look at me.

When we got to the field, I kissed my baby brother good-bye and waved to him until the car was out of sight. By then, Patrick was already halfway down the tire-track road. I ran to catch up, grateful for the warmth the exercise gave me.

"Everything seems so strange," I said to Patrick. "The bushes, the sounds. It even smells different today. Like it's a different part of the world." I glanced over at the dark towering hedge and couldn't help it—I shivered.

Al had on a yellow raincoat and his hands were squeezed into thick wool gloves, the kind with the tips cut off, so the tops of his fingers poked through like pale, fat worms. "Looks like rain today," he said, handing us our buckets. "Let's hope you can get something picked before it gets serious."

I said, "What happens when it gets serious?"

"You go up to the office. Bev will call your ride. Can't pick in the rain, the berries get too mushy. I'll put you on forty-seven today. Lucky forty-seven." And he winked.

Out in our row, the weight of the sky gave me a completely new feeling—it was like being in the middle of an ocean when the waves turned rough. No one was talking or yelling out jokes. I wondered if we were the only two out there. "Isn't it strange, Patrick?" I caught a glimpse of him through gaps in the bushes.

"What?"

"The feeling all around us. How gray the sky is. How the air is so heavy it almost *sounds* heavy, even though there's no sound at all."

"The best berries are farther in," Patrick said, skipping over the first bushes as quickly as he'd skipped over my words. "Let's try and get a big bucket filled before the rain starts. Like your old guy said." I heard the bushes shake and rustle as he barreled through the row.

"He's not *my* old guy!" But I understood why Patrick wanted to move ahead. Part of it had to do with that saying you hear: The grass is always greener on the other side of the fence. You would be standing in front of a bush and your eyes would wander, and it truly seemed that the bushes farther down the row were loaded with more berries than you'd ever seen. So you step down a bush or two and pick happily for a moment, but then your eyes would wander and the same thing would happen, all over again.

Then there was another part to it, though. Something

you would only know if you'd spent any time in a blueberry field. The truth was some bushes really *were* better than others. One bush might have a scattering of tiny, hard berries, while the bush right next to it would be loaded with enormous ripe clumps—berries that practically jumped into your bucket on their own. They were like people that way: pretty much the same but somehow completely different.

"Patrick," I called, trying to get the words out before I had completely formed the thought. "Patrick?"

"Yeah?"

"I'm starting to see bushes in a different way. I can't really explain it. They're living, though. They are alive, Patrick. Just like we are alive. And I really think they want to talk to me."

The sky rumbled and I thought I heard a giggle.

"Patrick?" I said, and I heard it again. It *was* a giggle.

I unhooked my little bucket and pushed through to Patrick's side of the row. I saw their feet before I saw the rest of them, standing just as close as two pairs of feet could possibly stand.

Patrick said, "We know you're there."

Shauna was wearing a clear plastic raincoat over a bright orange bikini top. She said, "I agree with you,

Melissa. I think all living things can communicate. That's why I don't eat certain vegetables."

"Right," I said. "That's stupid." And I pushed back through to my own side and tried to clear my mind of everything but the berries.

It must have worked, because when those first fat raindrops did fall, I was surprised. I looked up to judge the time, but without the sun, I couldn't tell. And I had no idea how long I'd been out there picking. Which makes me think that another secret of blueberries is the same as the secret of anything you love: It's easy to forget everything else.

"Patrick!" I called. "Let's get out of here."

But he didn't answer.

"Patrick?" I called again.

Ducking my head, I pushed through the row, stopping every few feet to listen for normal sounds of the field—a bucket clanging or a fuzzy radio.

There was nothing.

Nothing but the sound of rain bouncing off the leaves, so new and strange that my blueberry field didn't even feel like the same place anymore.

I didn't know which way to go. Should I walk the entire length of the row to make absolutely sure my brother wasn't there? Or should I give in to the knowing feeling that he was gone and head back to the weigh station?

I took another step down the row. And another. I called his name. And then I stopped and listened again, but all I heard was rain, pattering against the leaves.

I started to run. Branches smacked at my body, soaking me all the way to my skin. My little bucket bounced hard against my thigh, sending berries flying in every direction, but still, I didn't stop.

"Patrick!" I called again, even though I knew for certain. I'd made it all the way to the end of the row and he was gone.

Everyone was gone.

I ran all the way to the weigh station, where I found Al, wrapped in his yellow rain slicker. Even with his big sausage fingers and old man's nose, he looked as comforting to me right then as my own mother.

"I was just about to send the search-and-rescue in after you, Melissa," he said. "Your brother said you were right behind him but that was thirty minutes ago." He pried the wire handle of my bucket from my numb fingers and set it on the scale.

My clothes were plastered to my body. Wet hair stuck to my face. "Where is he?"

"Well, he weighed his berries, grabbed his lunch, and headed up to the office with the others."

I nodded. It all sounded so normal. But I *hadn't* been

right behind him. He would have had to sneak past me, or circle around me on another row. He would have had to work hard to give me the slip like that.

Al said, "You'd better scoot—I'm sure your mother will be driving up any minute, if she's not there already." He handed me the slip of paper with the number of pounds I'd picked, and also my lunch sack. "I'll see you when the sky dries out."

I couldn't speak. I turned and walked back up the tire-track road, which was now a mess of thick, dark mud. The parking lot was even worse: slick gravel and wide puddles, soggy paper lunch bags and drenched kids climbing into minivans. When I didn't see my brother or our car, I went to the office and stood shivering at the window. I cleared my throat and coughed and even faked a sneeze until Bev finally appeared.

"Hon! Look at you! Soaked to the skin! Your teeth are actually chattering, just like the young ladies in my books. They always manage to get locked out during a rainstorm, too."

I handed over my soggy scrap of paper and glanced back across the drive. "Have you seen my brother?"

"Sure. He was here with his buddies." She slid a few bills my way, and some change. I scooped it up without looking. I still didn't see Patrick.

Bev watched me for a moment and then stuck her head out the window to help me search. "There he is, hon. Right over there."

I followed her pointing finger to the corner of the lot, just in time to see Shauna opening the door to a silver minivan. Her orange bikini top showed through the clear plastic raincoat, which had started to fog up from the inside.

My brother was there, too, waving at her, and laughing, his hair slicked down over his forehead and his face shiny and flushed. My skinny brother, all elbows and knees, as Dad used to say. My skinny brother suddenly looked different to me. Standing there soaked and shivery, with his pale thin legs poking out through baggy wet shorts, he looked carefree. Radiant. And when I saw him looking like that, I realized something that made my heart ache.

As hard as I'd tried to pretend it wasn't happening, it was official: I had just lost one more thing in my life. Someone else had left me behind.

CHAPTER 18

WE SAT AROUND WATCHING OLD WESTERN RERUNS. We studied the sky for some sign of light, but the gray wouldn't budge and the rain didn't let up. When the TV weather guy shook his head and said, "We're socked in for a few days, folks," we dragged out the Scrabble board and the Yahtzee dice, made a few words and added up some numbers, but mostly Patrick and I just sat on opposite ends of the couch and stared at the black-and-white world of good guys and bad guys.

I waited for Patrick to say something—to explain or apologize, but he didn't. Maybe the memory of Shauna in that orange bikini top with her clear plastic raincoat fogging up from the inside was using all the space in his head.

But then, after another cowboy showdown, Mom finally had enough. She marched into the living room and snapped off the TV. She pointed to the far wall, at the paint strips that had been taped up so long ago that I'd almost forgotten they were there. "Get off the couch," she said. "Get over here."

"What?" Patrick asked. "What's going on?" His eyes were still fixed on the blank TV screen, making me wonder if Mom's warning about freezing our eyeballs with too much screen time had been right.

"What does it look like?" Mom asked. "What do you think? We're going to Disneyland?" Which I thought was pretty funny until Claude ran in squealing, "Middy Mouse, Middy Mouse!"

Mom scooped him up and kissed his fat cheek. "Oh, honey. Not really. There's no Mickey." She pointed to the wall. "But look. We're picking out a paint color for the living room. What do you think, Mr. Claude?"

Claude put his hand in his mouth and sucked on his fingers. "Yellow," he said finally. He grinned around the room, waiting for applause. When he didn't get it, he clapped for himself. "Yellow!" he shouted.

"They're all yellow, Claudie." I rolled off the couch and joined my mother at the wall. "They're all yellow, aren't they?"

I started reading the yellow names to myself: Fresh Butter, Lemon Meringue, Sun Porch, Sun-Kissed, Baby Chick, Atomic Light, Banana Cream, and, my favorite name, Just Plain Yellow. I couldn't imagine a room covered with any of them.

"How about that one." Patrick had managed to crawl out from his sunken nest in the couch, too. As he stood next to Mom, he tilted his head thoughtfully. "Banana Cream," he said finally, with certainty. It was the palest of the yellows, velvety soft.

"It's nice," Mom said. But she didn't sound sure. "Which one, Mr. Claudio? Which yellow do you like?"

Claude's sticky fingers reached out for Lemon Meringue, a color so blinding it reminded me of one of Shauna's bikini tops. I held my breath, hoping Mom wouldn't take advice from a person who sometimes forgot to use the toilet.

I took a step back and squinted, making the colors blend and stretch together in an electric, dizzying way. "I don't know, Mom," I said. "If you ask me, they're all extremely yellow."

We stood quietly for several more moments, contemplating yellow, yellow, *which yellow?* Mom suddenly reached out and snatched one off the wall. "This is it," she announced.

I leaned over and read, "Sun-Kissed. Are you sure, Mom?" It was actually the prettiest color on the wall, deep and rich, but it looked, well, loud. And bright. Nothing like any living room color I'd ever seen.

"I think it's lovely," she said.

Patrick cleared his throat. "But it doesn't really look like a room color, Mom."

I knew he was thinking of Dad's new old house, the warm-but-soft colors that blended perfectly and set a mood without shouting. This yellow, this Sun-Kissed, well, it shouted. And what were we shouting, anyway? What did we have to shout about?

Already Mom was peeling the other strips from the wall; for her, the decision had been made. Patrick insisted that Mom *at least* think carefully about the trim color. "If you make the trim too white, it will fight with the wall color. Some whites are actually more like yellows, but when they're on the wall, they look white. Some even have green undertones. You have to be careful."

What? Undertones? How did he know all this?

Mom went to the kitchen and came back with a stack of white paint samples. "Here," she said. "Help me decide."

Patrick flipped through the white strips, occasionally holding one up to her yellow sample. I gathered up the cast-off shades of white and spread them into a fan. Brilliant, Lancaster, Marshmallow, Montgomery, Sailboat, Linen, Bone, Cameo, and China. Patrick was right: white wasn't just white.

By the time we were in the car and on our way to the paint store to pick up our new living room colors (Sun-Kissed with Sailboat trim), Mom had decided that we should all bring home some new color samples to tape on our bedroom walls.

"A perfect project for later this summer," she said. "One room at a time." And in her voice was a lightness that made me feel, for a moment, anyway, something like hope.

CHAPTER 19

THAT EVENING WE PUT TAPE AROUND THE WINDOWS. It was good to be working, on my feet and moving my arms. After a quick dinner of scrambled eggs and honey toast, Mom asked me to put Claude to bed so that she and Patrick could start painting the trim. "I don't want to leave it half done," she said.

Sometime in the night I woke up and listened. Mixed with the splatter of rain sounds were noises coming from the living room—the soft shuffle of footsteps and the clank of a pail. I tried to get up and go help, but the bed was so warm that I snuggled deeper into the covers and drifted back to sleep. In the morning the trim was done.

Mom looked worn out but pleased. We were ready to start with the walls.

All that morning and into the afternoon, Patrick and I took turns either playing with Claude or helping Mom roll out long, smooth lines of Sun-Kissed Yellow. That evening, the walls in our living room had one coat of new paint. "It will look better with two coats, Mom," Patrick said kindly.

Mom just stared at the bright yellow walls with tired eyes.

She must have stayed up most of the night again, because on Wednesday morning the second coat was finished. We huddled together in the middle of the room, surrounded by paint fumes and the harsh glare of Sun-Kissed Yellow. The new color made everything feel strange, like we were being told to feel one thing when we all really felt something else.

I woke early Thursday morning to sun—actual sun—and I jumped out of bed, thinking of the blueberries. But when I saw Patrick in the hallway, dressed already, I said, "Where do you think you're going?"

"What do you mean? It's sunny."

"Yeah, but maybe I'll tell Mom about what you did to

me. How you left me out there. Maybe that will be the end of it for you."

"Then it will be the end for you, too," he said.

I shrugged, like I didn't care. Patrick waited a moment, then turned and walked to the kitchen to start making our lunches. I followed him, got the Mr. Coffee brewing, and pulled the box of cereal from the cupboard. Out of the corner of my eye I could see Patrick, glancing at me nervously. It made me feel powerful and strong.

I took out my 3-D glasses, which I'd tucked in my back pocket. I slipped them on, looked at him and smiled.

Patrick *hated* my 3-D glasses. But he didn't say a word. And while he spread jelly on two slices of bread, I peered through the empty frames. "Hmm . . . why are you doing *that*?"

He plunged a knife into the peanut butter and slopped it on the other two slices of bread. He squished the sides together. "Do you want an apple or a banana?"

I pushed the button for Spectacular Vision. "I think you're forgetting to say something to me," I said.

"Okay," Patrick said. "I'm sorry."

"It doesn't count if I have to ask for it."

"Missy, what do you want?" He still held a banana in one hand and an apple in the other.

I poured cereal and milk into my bowl. "I want you to tell Shauna to stay away."

"I'm not going to."

"Then we're not going to the field anymore."

"What do you have against her? She's really nice to you." Patrick's voice was normal, but his face was turning red.

"She's just, she's just—" I didn't know what to say. "She's trying to make trouble."

"Missy, no. Seriously. We're just having fun."

"Fun doing what?"

"Missy, the day in the rain. I knew you wouldn't come. I knew you'd probably tell Al. So that's why I went without you. We went exploring. We actually found a hole in the hedge that leads to the other field. Lyle's field. He's the brother—"

"I know that," I said. "I know who he is. I'm not dumb."

Mom's voice was suddenly right behind me, making me jump. "Who is saying anything about dumb? We don't use that word in this house." She stepped all the way into the kitchen, holding a sleepy Claude. When she saw Mr. Coffee all ready to go, she smiled. "Ah, thank you. Now, what were you two talking about?"

I stared at Patrick. He stared back at me. Finally he

answered. "I was just asking Missy if she wanted an apple or a banana."

I looked around the messy kitchen . . . even it smelled like wet paint. I said, "Well, I was just saying that bringing a banana in a paper bag is dumb. That's what is dumb. It gets bruised up."

"Right," Mom said absently. She poured herself a big cup of coffee. Patrick's mouth twitched into a victory smile. But he wasn't the winner. I would find a way to show him that.

"You're not going to wear those glasses in the field today, are you?" Patrick asked, shoving an apple into my lunch sack.

I'd actually forgotten I was wearing them. "Yes," I said. "Why?"

"Because you never know," I started, but kept the rest to myself. *You Never Know When You Need to See the World Clearly.*

CHAPTER 20

AL CHUCKLED WHEN HE SAW ME. "I SEE YOU HAVE A new look." Patrick glanced around nervously, and I knew he wanted to get out of there before anyone spotted me in my glasses. Ha!

"What row are we on today, Al?" I asked.

Al said, "Well, that's something I wanted to talk to the two of you about. I have some news for you—"

I held my breath, thinking of the prize. Even though hard work is its own reward, I knew there had to be something more. The ad in the newspaper said so.

Al said, "All that rain put us back a bit. Plus, the weather people say there's a big heat wave coming. So Moose is going to bring out the picking machine. He asked me to recommend a couple of responsible kids to work in the sorting shed. It's easier work and more money. I immediately thought of you two."

I looked at Patrick, waiting. He said, "Just us?"

"That's all we need."

Patrick shook his head. "Then, no. Not for me."

I pulled off my glasses and stepped closer to him. "But Patrick—think of the money. Think of the new clothes. This is a promotion!"

"Sorry, Missy. I'm not interested. But you can do it if you want."

"No—" I started. But then I thought about the day in the rain. I thought about Patrick and Shauna and the raincoat fogged up from the inside. About belly button dances and berry tosses and whispers and giggles and feet standing too close. About being left behind. Sure, I could stay and try to humiliate him with little sister things, like 3-D glasses and spying and stupid jokes. But he didn't care. So I would show him. I'd make more money and have more fun and he might even miss me. "Okay," I said, turning back to Al. "I'll do it."

Al glanced from my brother to me. "Are you sure?"

I swallowed the lump in my throat and nodded.

"Have fun, Missy," Patrick said. His voice was genuinely nice.

I couldn't look at him.

Al sent me back up the tire-track road. He told me to knock on the office window and tell Bev that I was the new sorter. I didn't pass Shauna or any other picker on the way back, which I was glad about, since I was trying my hardest not to cry.

The first thing Bev said was, "I was hoping it would be you. I'll call your mom for permission and then show you the ropes." She pushed a button and the garage doors creaked open. "Go on in. I'll be right back."

I stepped into what appeared to be a garage, except there were no cars or lawn mowers or bicycles or anything else that ordinary people had in their garages. Instead, there were stacks of different-sized buckets, wide wooden crates, bags of fertilizer, tractor parts, and, taking up most of the floor space, a long machine with a black rubber conveyor belt. Bev came back and made a big motion with her hand. "Welcome to our palace."

"What did my mom say?"

"She said it was fine."

"Even without my brother?" I was halfway hoping Mom would say I couldn't do it without Patrick. That we needed to stick together.

"She was proud of your promotion." Bev walked around the room, flipping on light switches and the overhead fan. She hoisted a crate to the front of the conveyor belt. "Here are some berries to get you started."

She poured berries in a tray at the front of the machine and then turned it on. It was so loud that all she could do was point and make motions, but I got the idea. There was a button to get the belt going and the same button stopped it. There was a lever to control the speed.

She turned it off to speak. "The picking machine doesn't pick clean. See this—" she held up a bunch of berries still clinging to a branch. "It grabs everything. It's your job to sort things out. The green ones and the rotten ones and the stems. You think you can do that?"

I eyed the machine nervously. "It's so big. And loud."

"You'll get used to it. I'll just be through that door, if you need me. Our kitchen is on the other side. There's a bathroom, too. Just go right on in when you need to use it."

I faced the enormous conveyor-belt machine with all its knobs and levers and metal and buttons. "I don't really know what I'm doing."

"Just get started, hon. It will all make sense once you do." And then she left me.

I turned back and pushed a button. The machine roared to life. My fingers were back to being clumsy, just like that first day of picking. Cars turned into the gravel drive, dropping kids off, and I saw them out of the corner of my eye. But the belt moved so fast I couldn't look away. *Green ones, rotten ones, stems, and whatever else doesn't belong.*

CHAPTER 21

IT WAS THE WORST MISTAKE EVER. MY BACK ACHED and my eyes were blurry. Sorting berries made my brain feel like it was swelling, and I was pretty sure that at any moment, my skull would explode from the pressure. Also, it was lonesome. I had this feeling that if I walked outside, I would discover that I was the only person left in the entire universe.

I was just about to turn off the machine and run back to the field when I felt a tap on my shoulder. There was Bev, holding two cans of soda and motioning to the on-off button. When I pushed it, the conveyor belt slowed to a stop, but my ears roared like it was still going.

"How about we go sit in the sun for a minute?" she

said. "It's coffee-break time. Grab a couple of buckets. Those white plastic ones are best for sitting."

I grabbed two big plastic buckets from the pile and followed Bev across the gravel drive, to a small tree and a patch of shade. I looked up to see the time. About ten o'clock, judging from the sun. It felt good on my face.

"This is where I take most of my breaks," Bev said, motioning me to set down the buckets. "Underneath this pretty cherry tree. Now you'll know all my secrets." She handed me the soda and I opened it quickly.

"Ahh," I said, after my first bubbly sip. "That's good."

"Hits the spot," she agreed. "So how's the sorting going for you?"

"Honestly," I said, "I don't think I can do this any longer."

She nodded. "It's hard work. Some people work on conveyor belts their entire lives. You know what the key is?"

I shook my head.

"A rich inner life. You know what that means?"

I shook my head again and took another sip of soda. It tingled deliciously.

"You just need to let your mind go somewhere else. Dream about the world and all the places you'd like to see. Your body might be stuck here, but your mind can go anywhere it wants." She pulled a paperback from her back pocket. "I like to travel this way, on horseback with Baron Von Handsome." She laughed. "But don't tell Moose."

"Okay," I said. I wondered about my own inner life. I closed my eyes but all I could see were Western shootouts and showdowns. Maybe Mom was right—maybe we *did* watch too much TV.

"So you think you can stick with it?"

"What?"

"This job. You think you can stick it out?"

I took a deep breath. "Well, I miss the berries already. I miss the field."

"You do, huh? I always hated it myself. Too claustrophobic for me, with all those bushes crowding around." She pretended to shiver. "What do you like about it?"

I took another drink and thought about slipping into the darkness of the row, hearing the sound of my own breath and watching my hands busy with work. "I guess I just like the bushes." I laughed, suddenly embarrassed.

She smiled. "Oh, you and Moose. Peas in a pod. Just watch yourself. You might grow up to be a farmer someday. And that's hard work."

"It doesn't look so hard."

"Trust me. It's hard." I glanced at her face. She was staring ahead, but she didn't seem to be seeing what was right in front of her. "You're doing a good job for us, hon. We appreciate it."

"Well, I love it here." And as I blurted it out I knew it was the pure truth.

"Moose loves it, too. He's a man of few words. I get seven words a day from him, if I'm lucky. But being a farmer means the world to him. I swear he talks to the bushes and the bushes talk back. Does that make any sense to you?"

"Yes." I felt the air go out of my lungs. "Perfect sense."

Bev smiled. "Back in the day all the kids were like you—real serious pickers and workers. We had grown-ups, too. Migrant workers who followed the seasons. We're not big enough for that anymore. Had to sell off some acreage we had near here. Sold it after, well—" she stopped and motioned to the hedge. Took another big gulp of her soda.

"So we'd been relying on the picking machine all these years, and that was fine. We had some good sorters for the machine, and it worked out well enough. Moose and I, we both take on odd jobs in the off-season, to make ends meet. But we don't mind. We've been doing it like this for years. Then this year, Moose went and changed everything. For some reason, he wanted kids back in the field. It came as a complete shock to me. He even put the ad in the *Little Nickel* without me knowing. All of a sudden one day, I start getting these calls. Parents telling me they saw the ad and thinking this would be a good option for their kids. I said, 'Whoa—what number are you calling?' I finally straightened it out with Moose."

She shook her head and took another long drink of soda. I thought she was done, but then she went on.

"So we had a good fight about it, me and Moose. I did all the yelling and he said his seven words, and then he set his jaw and that's when I knew he'd won. The whole time parents kept calling. This is cheaper than summer camp and most of them want their kids to learn how much work it takes to make a buck. And so"—she raised her can of soda to me, "here we are."

I thought about everything I'd learned already, picking berries. "I'm glad," I said, raising my can to clink with hers. "I'm glad Moose put the ad in the paper."

Bev shrugged. "Times have changed, but I guess we can try and hold on to the few precious things that haven't. I guess that's what Moose is trying to do."

I nodded. I liked how she was talking to me, like I was a real person to her.

She said, "Can you give me five minutes and help pick this cherry tree?"

"Sure!" I jumped up and ran to the garage for two metal picking buckets.

Picking cherries was different from picking blueberries. I found that out right away. But my fingers felt that good busyness, and my arms felt strong and useful, and the sun felt like a friend on my face.

Bev told me that they were pie cherries, not as sweet as regular eating cherries, and when I popped one in my mouth, it was soft and warm and tart. "Mmm," I said, working my teeth around the pit. "It's good. I've never picked a cherry before. But it's fun, too."

Bev laughed. "You're a different kind of kid." I couldn't see her face through the branches, but it sounded like she was giving me a compliment. "What other things do you like to do?"

Probably because my hands were flying over the tree like that, and we were working together, I felt free to talk. "Just regular things. I have a little brother and I help take care of him. I like to read. I like to ride my bike. And watch Westerns on TV. I have two best friends, but they're away at camp."

"Camp. Now that sounds fun. That's what you should be doing."

"No," I said. "I like this."

She laughed.

"No, really. I mean it. This is important."

"Important, huh?"

"Yeah." And then I heard myself telling her things, things I'd learned from being in the field, and other things, too. It felt good to talk like that. When I caught a glimpse of her between the thick green leaves of the cherry tree, I was almost surprised she wasn't Constance or Allie.

When I'd picked all the cherries I could reach by standing on my overturned bucket, Bev said, "I'll get Moose to get the ladder for me later. There is plenty here already for a pie."

I handed her my bucket, nearly full. "Maybe two pies," she said. "Listen, thank you for your help. I'll tell Moose what a nice talk we had today. Don't you worry— we'll get you back out there. We'll get you back picking."

"Thank you," I said. And I spent the rest of the day at the conveyor belt.

Maybe it was not having the sun over my head. Maybe it was the constant motion of the conveyor belt. Maybe it was the soda pop, which I wasn't used to, or the loneliness, especially when I took my lunch break and thought of my brother, making my sandwich. Or it could have been the hard work of coming up with a rich inner life, which is not as easy as it sounds. Whatever it was, by the time Mom picked us up, I didn't feel like myself. I didn't feel like Missy, or even Melissa. And I didn't feel like talking.

But I did have a paper bag of bright red cherries,

which was something special from the day. "Measured out for a pie," Bev had told me. She'd also given me her very own State Fair Award-Winning Cherry Pie Recipe.

"How was it?" Patrick asked from the front seat, halfway turning around. The windows were all rolled down, but the air was so hot it didn't even cool us off. "How much money did you make?"

I didn't answer. I pretended not to hear.

Mom glanced at me in the rearview mirror. "How much, Missy?"

"Twenty," I said flatly. "Twenty dollars."

Mom said, "That's fantastic!"

I waited for Patrick to say something, and when he didn't I wondered if he cared even the tiniest bit. Or if being with Shauna out there—without his tagalong sister to get in the way—was all he cared about.

"Mom," I said, when we were halfway home and a block from the Price Rite. "Do we have flour? And butter and sugar?"

"Yes, of course we do."

I looked down at the recipe. "Tapioca," I said. "Do we have that?"

"No."

"Then could we stop at the store?"

"What for, Missy?"

"I want to make a pie."

Everyone stayed in the car while I went in for the tapioca. I didn't know where I'd find it, so I walked up and down every single aisle. In the canned fruit aisle I slowed down. I couldn't help dragging my fingers along each can, studying the colorful pictures on the labels. Canned pineapple, canned peaches, canned pears, canned cherries and, finally, canned blueberries.

I pulled the blueberries from the shelf and turned the can over and over in my hand. There was a whole world inside that can. There was a farmer inside it, and pickers. There were bugs and bees and sun and rain. There was a radio playing and jokes being told.

I set it back, overwhelmed by the lights in the store, the crush of people with their metal shopping carts plucking brightly colored packages from the shelves, just as earlier in the day, I had plucked sun-warmed cherries from a tree.

I walked slowly back to the car. "I couldn't find it, Mom. I don't even know what it is." She told me to wait in the car with the boys. Three minutes later she returned with a box of tapioca.

"Are you really going to make a pie?" Patrick asked me.

"I'm going to try."

CHAPTER 22

Dear Constance and Allison,

Today I made my first ever pie. It was cherry.
I wish you could have been here to eat it. Here's what
you do: You get flour and put in a half teaspoon
of salt. Then you cut two cubes of butter into little
pieces and drop them in the flour. You can mix it up
with your fingers.

Then you get ice water. It has to be ice water.
So what's smart is to get the water ready with ice
cubes before you start doing anything else. You add
just enough ice water to make it all stick together.
But not too much or the dough will be tough.

So when the dough is just right and able to hold together, you divide it into two balls and wrap it up and stick it in the fridge. Then you get your cherries. Mine were fresh, straight from a tree, so I had to get the pits out. Claude helped with that part. Then you mix the cherries with sugar, a pinch of salt, and this stuff called tapioca, which makes it thicken up while it cooks. Some people use flour for thickening, but not in my recipe.

Oh, and before you do anything, you should turn the oven on so it will be the right temperature when everything is ready. And also before you put on the top crust, you put tiny bits of butter on top of the cherry mixture.

Rolling out the dough was the hardest part. Mine fell into pieces and stuck to the counter, but I just sort of pulled it up and pressed it into the pie dish. The top didn't look so good, but in the end it tasted fine. Actually, it tasted delicious. I sort of didn't want to eat it because it was so perfect, just sitting there. But then the smell got to me. Plus everyone was begging for a piece, and Claude started to hit me and yell that it was his pie and he made it so he should

*eat it and not share with anyone. That was
funny. We ate half of it right away. It was still
warm even.*

*The weather has been sunny, but I haven't
gone down to the lake so I haven't seen BM
or anyone else. It wouldn't be fun without you
anyway, so we'll go when you get back. Nothing
much more is happening around here except
we painted the living room yellow which is
kind of weird. Anyway, I hope you are having
fun. When you get back I'll show you how to
make a pie.*

*Your Friend,
Missy*

I'd almost signed Melissa but caught myself just in time. They didn't know about Melissa. Plus, Melissa would have told them about the blueberry field and the tiny farmer named Moose and the fight called a blood feud. About Al and the voices and how Patrick liked Shauna. About being left in the rain. She would have told them it was Bev who had explained about making the crust, as well as sharing her State Fair Award-Winning Cherry Pie Recipe.

Melissa would have also told them about her father's upcoming wedding.

No, actually. Missy would have told them that. But it was all too much for a letter. It would have to wait until they came home.

CHAPTER 23

THE NEXT MORNING, AFTER MOM DROPPED US OFF, Patrick followed me to the garage. The doors were closed and the lights off. "What? Did you change your mind?" I couldn't hide my excitement.

Patrick said, "So you really like this?"

"Sure. It's great. Bev gave me a soda yesterday." I pointed to the overturned white buckets. "Under that cherry tree. It's really fun. And you'll make more money."

Patrick looked at me closely. "Did she tell you anything?"

"Sure. She told me a lot of things." I was so happy I was practically jumping.

"Anything about Moose and Lyle?"

"What? No. She told me how to make that pie. Let's go find her. I know she'll want you to work on the other side of the conveyor belt. There's a heat wave coming, and we can make it go faster and sort more berries and—"

Patrick said, "Missy, don't you wonder why the farmers split the field? Don't you wonder about the giant hedge? Why they won't talk to each other?"

My heart was starting to beat faster, but in a different way. A warning way. "The blood feud?" I said.

"Exactly. There's something out here, Missy. Something Moose has that Lyle doesn't. Have you seen anything? Heard anything?"

I looked down at our feet, planted in the gravel. "That's why you're standing here talking to me right now?"

"What?"

I turned my back to him. "I have work to do."

"Missy, we're still doing our jobs. We're still picking berries. But we're having fun, too. We found a bird's nest, and there are these raccoons—"

"Seriously. Go before I tell on you."

"Tell what?"

"Tell Bev how you and your friends are snooping around. Tell Mom about the way you left me in the rain."

He didn't answer, but when I heard the gravel crunch,

I turned back to see him disappear around the corner of the garage. Quietly, I followed, just enough to watch him walk down the hill, a small cloud of dust at his feet. I looked for his limp and when I didn't see it, wondered if he was changing. Or was he just trying extra hard to walk straight? Whatever it was, I could see that something was different.

Once he was out of sight, I turned back to the sorting shed. I pushed the button to raise the doors. Inside, I flipped on all the lights, just as Bev had shown me. Next to the machine were flats of berries, already stacked, waiting to be sorted. I got started right away and soon enough, the strange new rhythm of the sorting machine made me forget everything else.

I was just finishing my last crate of berries when I felt a tap on my shoulder. I looked up to see Bev, standing with a soda in each hand. "Looks like you're getting the hang of it," she said as we crossed the gravel drive to our overturned white buckets underneath the tree. I popped the tab to my soda and watched the bubbles sputter up through the small hole.

The first sip was sweet and cold and perfect and made my voice come back to life. "I completely lost track of time," I said, squinting up at the sun.

"That means you've found your rich inner life."

I nodded. "And I finished sorting all the crates, too."

"You did? That's record time. Moose will be happy to hear."

"Will he be back soon with more?"

"Probably. You can just hang out here until he does."

"Okay," I said. We sat in silence together, listening to the buzzing and humming and chirping sounds. Birds hopped and swooped all around us, diving in for the ripe cherries near the top of the tree.

"Oh yeah," I said, suddenly remembering. "I made that pie yesterday."

"You did?" Bev sounded delighted. "Well! How was it?"

"I followed your recipe exactly, and it was the best pie in the world." I thought about the simple moment of measuring flour and salt with butter and water, rolling out the crust. "I let my little brother take the pits out of the cherries, and then he didn't think he should share it with anyone."

Bev chuckled. "My crust got a little too brown. I usually put a strip of tinfoil around the edges, but I was in a rush and didn't bother. The rest of it was good, though. Moose finished off the last half for breakfast this morning. He loves pie."

"Well." I cleared my throat, pretty sure that if I said

one more word about pie I would instantly turn into a fifty-year-old woman. "I was wondering about something." I paused, trying to get my courage up. "There's been some talk," I said.

"Hmm?"

"You know. The two farms. Moose and his brother."

When Bev didn't answer I started to get a sick feeling in the pit of my stomach. Her face was a straight-ahead statue, making me know I'd said the absolute wrong thing.

I filled my mouth with bubbly soda so I wouldn't start to babble again and ruin everything even more. When that wasn't enough and the silence was about to make my head explode, I reached into my back pocket and pulled out my 3-D glasses. I adjusted them on my face.

Then Bev laughed, and my head went back to normal. "You're missing some lenses," she said.

"My best friends and I fixed them up like this and started wearing them at school. It was really fun, even though some people laughed at us. But I have a feeling my friends won't wear them next year."

Bev said, "Why?"

"Because. Just because."

Bev said, "You're at that age, aren't you? That age when everything changes."

I nodded but couldn't look at her. In the silence I heard birds again, and crickets and bees. I took in a deep breath and smelled dirt and heat and grass. I said, "I was lonely in the blueberry field, but at least I had the bushes. Maybe while I wait for Moose I could go down and pick some more?"

When Bev spoke again, her voice was different. "Moose is worried. He thinks some of the kids are sneaking around, looking for—" she stopped. I waited for more but all she said was, "Do your friends' glasses look like that, too?"

"Not exactly. They're decorated. But we all decorated them differently. We all have this, though." I reached up and pushed the midnight blue Spectacular Button. There, on the gravel right in front of me, was a tiny ant carrying a twig three times his size. "Look at that!" I said, pointing.

Bev kept still. I glanced over and saw that she was watching me. Her face, in Spectacular 3-D, was something else. She was like the heroine on the cover of one of her romance novels. She smiled and I smiled back. For real.

"Okay, Melissa," she said. "Can you keep a secret from the other kids?"

I nodded.

"They can't find out," she said. "It's very important."

She put her soda can on the ground and stomped it with her foot. "Grab some picking buckets," she said. And as she turned and headed for the house I heard her say one more thing. She said it under her breath. She said, *"I sure hope Moose won't feed me to the dogs for this."*

CHAPTER 24

SOMETIMES THE BIGGEST SURPRISES ARE HIDDEN under the plainest wrapping. That's what I was thinking when Bev led me to the very back corner of the sorting garage, to a faded wooden door, a door I'd never noticed before. She opened it and stepped outside. "Welcome to our palace grounds," she said, sweeping her arm in a fancy way. And I did my best to hide my deep disappointment.

On a patchwork of dirt and brown grass, a rusting metal lawn chair lay next to a broken-down barbecue. There was a purple croquet ball, half buried in the dirt, next to the handle of a broken mallet, and an outdoor umbrella that had lost all its fabric and was just a skeleton of bare-bones wires. It was the saddest backyard in the history of backyards, like it belonged to people who once tried to have a good time but could never really get the hang of it.

Bev sighed as we stepped off the porch and walked past the broken rusted things. "Watch you don't poke yourself," she said, and I moved carefully around the spiky umbrella.

As soon as I passed all the junk, I noticed the hedge. "The hedge is even back here?" I asked, surprised.

"The hedge is everywhere." She turned and bent down close. "We had to hide it."

"What?"

Her voice stayed low. "What I'm going to show you. We had to move it from one location to another. This was long ago." She pointed to a section at the base of the hedge where an opening had been cut out, like a tiny gnome door. "Go ahead, hon."

"What?" I asked, surprised. "Go in there?"

"You'll have to bend down some. Squish yourself up. Careful of the prickles."

Her voice was so matter-of-fact that I didn't question it. I just turned sideways, crouched down, and eased my way through the opening. Bev was right behind. When I straightened up on the other side, I found myself standing on a small pathway, in the middle of two halves of the hedge. Bev pushed past me saying, "I'll lead the way."

Walking along the dirt path, in between two massive hedges, the buckets in my hand were the only things that seemed normal, so I held on tight. We walked in a straight line, or at least that's how it seemed. It was like one of those mazes cut out of hedges, the ones on the grounds of fancy English country houses. But I didn't say that to Bev. I didn't know what to say.

As though she'd read my mind, Bev announced, "The first trip out always seems the longest." A moment later she stopped. "Here it is." And that's when I saw another opening cut into the hedge. Another gnome door.

Bev went first and I squeezed in behind her. But this time when I stood up, I found myself in a small meadow. There were golden grasses, waving in the breeze, and tiny wildflowers of every color. Fat round bumblebees rolled lazily from one sweet spot to another. I took in a deep breath and could tell that somewhere, very close by, dark, juicy blackberries were starting to bake in the late-morning sun. Every blade of grass, every clump of dirt—I could see it all so clearly, the way things get when the world stops making sense.

"It's beautiful," I said softly. "Like a magical place."

Bev nodded. "Think of it as our real backyard. Who needs a fancy lawn chair, right?"

"Right," I said.

"Now, listen. What I'm about to show you we keep as secret as we can, but that's not saying much." She shook her head. "There's a restraining order out on Moose's brother. It means if he steps over here, he is officially breaking the law. Now, hon, I'm not trying to burden you with grown-up troubles, but I'm just trying to let you know how special it is. Before I take you there, I want to make sure you understand."

"A restraining order?"

"It's an old, long story. And I'm not asking you to keep a secret from your mom or dad. But I'd appreciate it if you'd use some discretion with your brother and the other kids out here."

"Okay," I said.

Bev started walking again, through the tall golden grasses and sweet-smelling wildflowers, and I followed. When we got to the edge of the meadow, she stopped. In front of me was an enormous stretch of powdery-white sand, as long and as wide as at least one football field.

"How'd this sand—" I started to ask, and then I noticed the plants. Growing in the sand were bushes, rows and rows of low-lying, bright green bushes. They looked familiar, but completely strange, too. I took a step closer and suddenly understood. The plants, they were blueberry bushes, impossibly tiny blueberry bushes. And they were growing in sand.

I took another step. "So this is it? The big secret?"

"This is it," Bev answered quietly. "Like I said we had to move this entire field once, plant by plant and truckloads of this special sandy soil. This new location, no one else has ever been. The hedge helps keep it hidden. The berries are perfect right now, and they need to be picked. You'll be alone out here, but don't worry—if anything spooks you, just come back the way we came. Through the hedge and straight to the back of the house. You can do that, can't you?"

"Yes," I said. I set down my big bucket and slipped the wire of the five-pound can into my belt loop.

"There's one more thing." She held up her hand, motioning me to listen. From somewhere, not too far away, I heard a sound. Laughter? A radio? Bev pointed across to the far side of the field. That's when I noticed something I hadn't at first. The giant hedge surrounded me on all sides. I was completely boxed in.

She said, "That's the field. The big field."

"What? You mean with Al? And my brother? And all the pickers?"

"That's right. Just over there. On the other side of the hedge. You'll be able to hear the kids sometimes. When they get too close."

I must have walked past this little field every morning, never knowing what was on the other side of the hedge. "So wait—they're right over there?"

"Al tries to keep them on the far side of the field, but as you know, sometimes kids have a tendency to wander."

"It's so strange," I said quietly, afraid of being heard.

Bev said, "Just remember, this is a special field of berries. We call it the Little Field, and it means the world to Moose. I know I should have asked him first, but the berries need picking and I have a good feeling about you. Like I said, any time you need, come back the way you came. Understand?"

I nodded.

She pointed to small wooden building in the far corner of the field. "The outhouse here is nice and clean. Not like the one in the main field. You'll have it all to yourself. So what do you think? You okay here? You want to give it a whirl?"

I nodded again. "I'll give it a whirl."

"Just do your best. Moose will be out to check on you later." And then she said something more, something Bev-like and cheerful, but all I remember was that when she turned and crossed the meadow, I was alone.

I'd felt alone before. But I'd never felt alone and been alone at the same time. It made me think that maybe I wasn't real. Like if I didn't take a step, I might disappear. Or if I did take a step, I might fall off the edge of the world.

I imagined those brave people who set sail, back when they believed the world was as flat as a table, setting sail into nothingness and thinking that if a wind blew in the wrong direction, they might simply slip over the edge. And into what? Floating darkness? What else could they have imagined? What else could there have been?

If I don't move soon, I might not be able to move. And then what would happen? Would Bev come looking and find me standing where she'd left me, bucket in hand, baked solid from the sun? If she reached out and touched me, would I crumble down upon myself into a dry heap of sand? Was that why these bushes were here, growing in sand? Was this one of those fairy tales where the kids get turned into something else—a rock, a candy doorknob, a small pile of dust? A blueberry bush?

Move, I said to myself. *Move, Missy. Move, Melissa.*

I took a step. My foot sank into the smooth, sandy soil. I picked up my other foot and set it down. Then, towering over the first bush, I reached out my hand and cupped a handful of berries. And the moment I did, everything, suddenly, made absolute perfect sense.

I knew right then I'd done it. I had just won the prize.

CHAPTER 25

AT FIRST I COULDN'T SHAKE THE IDEA THAT THIS really was a fairy tale—the one where, no matter how much porridge you ate, the magic pot was still always full. The strange bushes were small, but they were loaded with the most amazing berries I'd ever seen, blueberries from another time, like maybe when dinosaurs roamed the earth. And the moment I thought I'd picked every berry on a bush, hunched over like an awkward giant, another clump—round and smooth and big as quarters—suddenly appear from underneath a soft, green leaf.

I picked slowly, trying not to disturb the enormous berries that were just waiting for a few more days of sun. But even though I was picking slowly, my little bucket was full almost immediately. The berries were that big!

Carefully, I unhooked the wire from my sagging belt loop and carried it to the big buckets I'd left by the hedge. I scooped out handfuls of berries and placed them in the bottom of the big bucket. Then I tucked the bucket close to the hedge, out of the sun, and went back to work.

I had no idea how long I'd been picking when I looked up to see a kid standing at the edge of the meadow, right next to the small opening. I let out a yelp. Then I realized it wasn't a kid at all. It was Moose.

When he saw that he'd been spotted, he crossed the meadow and came right up to me. "Sorry," he said quietly. "I guess I should have whistled or something."

Even though I'd seen him that one time before, I wasn't prepared for the shock of Moose up close. For one thing, his body was the size of a kid, but his face was old and weathered. Weathered is the way I've heard faces described but I'd never understood it until that first time of seeing Moose. It meant a face that had stayed out in the sun and wind and rain too long, until it ended up like an apple or potato or pumpkin skipped over during harvest.

I tried not to stare as Moose tipped back the brim of his hat. It was a farmer's hat, bright green with a picture of a yellow deer, or something with antlers. I waited for him to say something, anything, and when he didn't, I turned back to the bushes. My fingers were stiff with trying so hard to pick just right.

I thought about what Bev had said, about the fact that Moose only used about seven words a day. Something about Moose made me feel embarrassed, like I didn't know quite where to look. So I just continued to pick until my belt loop sagged again from the weight of the picking bucket. That's when Moose stepped up and handed me an empty pail.

"They fill up fast out here. I'll take your big ones in. I brought your lunch. And Bev sent a soda."

I hadn't been thinking about lunch or a soda, but when I saw my brown paper sack and the frosty can, I realized how empty my stomach was, and that my throat was scratchy-dry. Moose glanced back at the two big buckets near the hedge, the ones I'd already filled. "You put them in the shade," he said. "That's the right thing to do. Probably the best place for eating, too. Get your head out of the sun."

I took my sack and soda, walked over to the shade, silently counting how many words Moose had just used. I popped the tab on the soda. "Tell Bev thanks for me."

Moose didn't answer, just stood a few feet away, shuffling back and forth. Maybe he didn't think I was picking fast enough. Maybe he'd send me back to the sorting shed. Quickly, I pulled out my sandwich and took a huge bite. I'd eat my lunch fast and get straight back to the field. He'd see what a good worker I was.

"Well, I'll tell you something else." The way he said it was like we'd been chatting nonstop for the past three hours. I stopped chewing and looked up.

"What?"

He pushed back his cap again and rubbed his forehead, smearing a patch of sweat and dirt. "These berries," he said, "are shipped to two places. One is a restaurant in France that I can't tell you the name of—mostly because I can't pronounce it. And the other is to a millionaire's mansion in Kentucky."

"Oh." I realized my mouth was still full of sandwich. I reminded myself to chew and swallow.

"They fetch a pretty penny."

"Oh," I said again. As I watched his face looking out over his field, I could tell there was something more he was trying to say—something worth using up his quota of words on.

"Have you tried one yet?" he asked.

I shook my head.

"Go ahead. Try one."

I reached over and chose a berry from the top of my

bucket. I put it in my mouth and let it sit there a moment before biting down. When I did, the skin burst open with an amazing pop. I thought I had already tasted the best berries in the world, but this was something else. It was pure, sweet flavor, straight from a living bush, straight from the living earth, straight from someone's care and tending and love. I could taste all that, just like I could with the berries in the other field, but something about this berry was different.

I looked up at Moose. Looked him straight in the eye. I didn't feel the least bit shy anymore. "I've never tasted anything so good," I said. "So pure and good."

Moose's face turned like the sun. He smiled and looked out over his little field of berries. "It's the soil and the air and the sun and the honeybees," he said. "It's how everything lines up in the perfect combination. They are one in a million, these tiny bushes."

Then he took a small paper bag from the back pocket of his overalls and stepped into the field. He quickly filled the bag and handed it to me. "Here," he said. "A present for you. When you eat them, think about this. You are eating these before that millionaire in Kentucky and all those fancy-pants in France."

I laughed out loud. He looked startled for a moment, and then he laughed, too. We laughed together, like we were old friends, and that's when I knew this was my job for good.

"Would you like to come back? Or is it too lonely for you?"

I didn't want to tell him that I was already lonely, and being lonely around people was just about the worst feeling a person could have. "It's not too lonely at all," I said.

"Bev assured me you wouldn't go telling the other kids all about it."

"I won't." But even as I said it I was wondering: How could I hold it over my brother and keep it a secret at the same time?

I spent the rest of the afternoon trying to figure out a way.

The ride home was quiet until Claude got tired of being in the car, and he started to whine and squirm. I opened my paper bag of blueberries and popped one into his mouth. "Big," he said, his eyes round with surprise. "Big boo-berries."

"Yes, big ones." I watched the back of Patrick's head, daring him to turn around. I handed Claude another berry from the brown paper bag. He held it to his eye before eating it.

"More," he said. I handed him the entire bag, which kept him happy and quiet the rest of the trip.

If only Patrick would turn around, I thought. *Turn around, Patrick, and I'll show you the most precious berries in the world. Turn around, Patrick, and you can taste them, too. Turn around, Patrick. Turn around.*

But he didn't. And I knew I couldn't say the words out loud.

CHAPTER 26

BECAUSE DAD WAS AT A FROZEN TREAT CONVENTION and wouldn't be back until late on Friday, he and Tessa picked us up on Saturday afternoon. I thought maybe Claude would come, too, but Mom had already made other plans for him. Dad wasn't too happy about that.

When I got into the backseat, right away I smelled something good. "What's that?" I asked.

"Fried chicken and buttermilk biscuits," Dad said. "Picnic anyone?"

"Great," said Patrick. I didn't say another word.

Dad drove to a park that had a playground, apple trees just right for climbing, and plenty of wide-open patches of soft green grass. I wondered if they'd chosen it thinking we'd have Claude with us.

Tessa looked around for the perfect place and finally decided on a shady spot underneath one of the trees. As she rolled out a thick blanket and set it with cloth napkins and silverware, I stood and looked up at the small green apples, wondering how long until they would be ripe.

Dad pulled food from a giant bag. "How's this?" he asked, placing a bucket of fried chicken and a box of buttermilk biscuits in the middle of the blanket. There was also a container of mashed potatoes, a bottle of sparkling pink lemonade, a bowl of deep red cherries, and a plate piled high with chocolate-frosted brownies.

"It looks great," Patrick said. He sat down and took the plate Tessa held out for him. I settled on the grass and snatched a drumstick from the bucket, ignoring Tessa and her plate.

"Claude would have liked this," I said.

Usually the things that came out of my mouth were planned and calculated and meant to pierce Dad's heart, or to remind Tessa that there was another one of us— three all together! But this time I really meant it. This time, I simply missed my baby brother.

"Next time," Tessa said quickly. "It would be more fun with him here."

Something in the way she said it made me soften toward her, just for a moment. It was Mom, after all, who had started the thing in the Parenting Plan, about Claude needing to sleep in one place. And maybe he did, back then when they first split up. But he was older now. He would probably be fine. So maybe Dad was right when he got mad about it. Who was right? *Was* there a right? I dropped my drumstick on the blanket and rested my head in my hands.

"Are you feeling okay, Sport?" Dad asked.

"Yeah." I didn't look up. "Just tired." The truth was, right then my head felt as heavy as a bowling ball.

Dad set down his plate. He came right next to me and put his hand on my shoulder. "I know this is hard, Missy. I know you miss your brother when we're not all together. I do, too. And your mom thinks he's just about ready to spend the night away from her."

I smiled a little, thinking about how Claude liked to slide around on the shiny wooden floors at Dad's house. He liked his bedroom there, too, with little blue sailboat wallpaper, just waiting.

But as much as I looked forward to the time when he would spend the entire weekend in his room at Dad's new old house, it also made me ache. The idea of Mom, home alone with her bare yellow walls and abandoned toys, was just about the saddest thought ever. I suddenly realized the problem. No matter where I was, I would always be missing something. There was just no way around it.

The next morning, when I went downstairs, the sun was at its nine o'clock mark, the breakfast dishes were already in the dishwasher, the countertops had been wiped shiny-clean, and stacks of lavender-colored envelopes were piled on the table. I picked one up and pulled out the matching card inside.

Tessa Marie Johnston &
Theodore Edward McKenzie
Invite you to share and celebrate their wedding
Saturday, August 24
At 4:30 in the afternoon

Ugh. What would happen if the pretty cards disappeared? Maybe fell into a ditch or went down the toilet? What if I volunteered to drop them off at the post office, but they mysteriously got lost? What if Tessa Marie Johnston and Theodore Edward McKenzie threw a wedding and no one came? Would they still get married?

Or what about this: What if I readdressed them all, with random names from the phone book. What if on their wedding day, all these crazy strangers started showing up. What would they do then?

Shuffling through the stack, I examined the names and addresses on the cards. Some I knew, some I didn't. There was a whole section with the name Johnston, all from Ohio.

I had met Tessa's parents once—they'd given me a souvenir spoon from their hometown of Cleveland and were actually pretty nice without trying too hard. But suddenly, for the first time, I actually thought about a new *family* in my life. I would officially have step-people. Step-grandma and step-grandpa, step-uncles and aunties. Step-cousins, even. And I would be a step-person to all of them. It was enough to make a person's head explode.

Where was everyone, anyway? I needed to warn Patrick about the step-people who were about to invade our lives. "Patrick?" I called.

No answer.

I stood still and listened. And then I heard it: laughter from outside. I ran to the window and looked out. There were the three of them, busy at work moving enormous rocks, trimming trees, pulling weeds, and planting flowers.

I studied the yard, looking for a high spot to hide a bucket. What about that? A bucket of ice water, crashing down on their heads, right as they stared into each other's eyes and said, "I do."

Through the window I watched as Patrick held up a flowering red plant. Tessa pointed to the corner of the yard, and he trotted off like a stupid dog. It was bad enough watching my dad and Tessa prepare the backyard for their big, beautiful day, but knowing that Patrick was helping them—and laughing with them—was just too much. It made me dizzy.

My friend Constance would say that dizziness was the physical result of losing a life anchor. It was the kind of thing she said to me a lot when my parents were first splitting up. It made me laugh back then, even through my piercing pain and spinning head. This time, though, I wondered if maybe she was right. She and Allie were at camp, my mother was home with Claude, and Patrick, the one and only anchor I had at my father's house, was no longer an anchor.

I pictured a boat bobbing around on the wide-open sea. The more I thought about water and waves and boats, the dizzier I became. I thought back to the day they'd announced their plan to get married. Tessa's crab hand and her maid of honor question. She'd even bought the dress, without waiting for me to say yes. Without knowing my favorite color!

Well, I still hadn't said yes. And I wouldn't wear the dress.

But just thinking about it—just remembering that the dress was somewhere in the house—made me want to find it. Maybe I would destroy it. Cut it into tiny pieces. That would show them.

Slowly, because I was still dizzy, I started my search downstairs, in the hall closet where Patrick had seen it. It wasn't there.

I went up to my dad's room and searched his closet. It wasn't there, either. I knew it wouldn't be in Patrick's closet, so I didn't even bother looking. But, swallowing a lump in my throat, I did look in Claude's sailboat-wallpaper room. Not there.

Really, there was only one other place it could be, and that, of course, was the place I should have started.

CHAPTER 27

IT WAS SILVER-GREEN AND SHIMMERING, WITH PERFECT little crystal buttons running down the back. If it had been a gift, it would have been the nicest I'd ever received. And it had been in my closet all along. I just never looked in my closet, or even put clothes there. That would be too much like admitting it was permanent. That Dad's new old house was also my home.

I don't remember what I was thinking when I pulled the dress out and held it to my chest. What I do know is this: Somehow I was wearing it. Somehow my cutoffs and T-shirt were on the floor and the silvery-green maid of honor dress had slipped around me in the most perfect way, and I was wearing it and feeling like a princess, whichever one was fairest of them all.

I twirled around and felt the heavy silk cool against my legs. I twirled the other way and listened to the whispery sound it made.

My bedroom didn't have a full-length mirror, but the bathroom did. After first peeking out to make sure the coast was clear, I dashed across the hallway. I closed the bathroom door and turned to study the dress, how the silk billowed and floated as I moved. I twirled around and then twirled again. It was like a ride I couldn't get off. I was mid-twirl when the bathroom door opened and Patrick pushed inside.

"Oh, sorry!" He held up his hands, which were covered in dirt. "I didn't know you were—" And then he stopped, taking it all in. Me. The dress. Me wearing the dress.

"Wow," he said after a moment. "You look amazing."

"Haven't you heard of knocking?" I tried to step past him to run back to my room, but he didn't budge.

"That dress—it looks so good on you, Missy."

"Move!" I said, finally pushing him out of the way. I stumbled into the hallway just as Dad and Tessa appeared at the top of the steps. I wanted to shout, *This is a joke!* But nothing came out. So we all just stood in the hallway, staring.

"My goodness, Missy! I'd give you a hug but—" Dad motioned to the dirt on his hands. "Look at you! Look at my little girl!" He took a step toward me, and that broke the spell. Without a word, I turned and ran to my room. I slammed the door shut and locked it, too.

"Missy!" Tessa called. She knocked softly. "Missy, the dress is beautiful on you."

All the mean words I wanted to yell back at her were battling with these odd feelings of gratitude. Tessa *had* picked out a beautiful dress for me. And all three of them had stood there and given me such nice compliments, such shining looks. For a moment, I had been part of all their happy planning. I hadn't been alone.

But no. I wasn't part of it. I didn't want the wedding, and I *was* alone. And I would not wear a dress that Tessa picked out for me. I wouldn't.

I slipped out of the dress and left it in a shimmering heap on the floor, *where it belonged.* Then I grabbed my own clothes—my faded T-shirt and cutoff shorts. After I was dressed, I perched on the edge of the bed and waited to feel like myself again. But the feeling wouldn't come. My heart was still racing like it wasn't my own. Maybe the dress had cast some evil spell on me. Evil stepmother, evil spell.

Through the closed door came soft murmurs, and

then I heard my dad say something like, *"Maybe you can talk to her."*

The crumpled dress seemed to stare at me. Finally, I tiptoed over and picked it up. Remembering the silky whisperings and twirling ride, I felt a pang of sadness as I slipped it back on the hanger.

"Missy!" *Knock, knock, knock.* "Missy, it's just me. Patrick. Dad and Tessa went downstairs. Let me in. I want to talk to you."

"Go away, Patrick. I just want to be alone."

I hated that they'd all seen me wearing the dress. It felt like somehow they'd won. I hung the dress in the very back corner of the empty closet. If I had another dress in there, something completely ugly and hideous, I would put it on. I would put it on and stomp out into the hallway and say, "Here I am. Here I am in the dress I'm wearing to your wedding." And I laughed out loud, just thinking about it.

Then I stopped laughing.

I'd been trying to come up with a plan. A plan to ruin their wedding. And at that very moment, remembering their three happy faces beaming at me in a silvery-green maid of honor dress, I suddenly had one.

I yanked open the door. Patrick, who had been leaning against it, stumbled into the room.

"Missy—" he started, but I didn't let him finish.

"Tell them I'll wear it," I said quickly. "Tell them I'll be in the wedding and I'll wear the dress."

"Really?" Patrick said. It might have been my imagination, but a look that seemed like disappointment flickered across his face. Just for a moment, anyway.

"Yes," I said. It was the hardest thing I'd ever done, telling Patrick such a huge lie. So I forced myself to remember him in the backyard, just minutes before, helping them plant flowers and move boulders. "Tell them."

It was the day Dad and Tessa moved into full steam ahead wedding. Tessa even tried to get me to go to the mall with her and pick out shoes to wear with my silvery-green dress. I convinced her that I had the perfect shoes at home, and that I'd bring them next weekend so that she could see for herself.

"But what if the dress needs to be altered?" She frowned down at her wedding planning calendar. "You should try it on again."

"It fit perfectly. You saw it." It was actually a little loose and a little long, but with my plan, it wouldn't matter a bit.

"Okay," she said hesitantly. "Bring your shoes next weekend and we'll take another look at the dress. Are you sure it wasn't too loose in the waist?"

"Oh, no," I said. "It was like a glove. You saw it." And I even smiled.

As she nodded, surprised and grateful, I saw her replace the picture of the slightly loose-around-the-waist dress in her mind with the just-right one I'd handed her. Her lovely eyebrows went back to their normal places, she crossed off another item on her wedding to-do list, and she breathed a sigh of relief. *Because, after all, the wedding was just a few weeks away.*

I knew I couldn't stop it from happening, but I *could* stop it from being the glorious day of their dreams. In their perfectly landscaped world, I would be the one thorny weed.

CHAPTER 28

FIRST THING AFTER DAD DROPPED US HOME, I BEGGED Mom to take me shopping.

"What do you need, Missy?"

"Just some stuff. And will you take me to the mall instead of Second Time Around?"

She thought for a moment. "How about we all go right now? A special family outing? We can have dinner at the food court."

"Great," I said, while at the exact same time Patrick said, "No."

"Why not, Patrick?" I asked.

"I'm too tired."

"Right," I said. I knew the real reason. He was embarrassed to be seen with us.

Mom said, "Well, maybe you can stay home and watch Claude for us. Missy and I can have some girl time. How does that sound, Missy?"

"Great, Mom."

Patrick said to Claude, "We'll play duck-duck-goose as soon as they leave. Just us boys." Claude wiggled like an overjoyed puppy and even Patrick looked happy.

My mom went to her room and came out wearing a flowery skirt and pink blouse.

When I saw her I asked, "Should I change?" I was wearing my usual cutoffs and a T-shirt. My blueberry money was wadded up in my backpack.

"You look perfect, honey." To Patrick she said, "Just warm up some leftover macaroni and cheese for dinner."

On the road, Mom messed with the radio for a minute. Then she snapped it off and said, "I'm glad it's just us, Missy. I've wanted to take you shopping. I think it's time to buy you a bra."

My heart stopped. I clutched at it, convinced this was a heart attack. "What? No! I don't need a bra! Mom, if you're going to buy me a bra we can turn the car around and go home right now."

Mom laughed. "Missy, getting a bra is just part of life. It's part of growing up."

"But I'm not growing up, Mom. I'm having a heart attack. Turn the car around. Please!"

"Okay, listen. No bra today." She glanced over at me and shook her head, but she was smiling, too. "What is it you wanted to buy?"

"I want a dress."

"What kind of dress?"

"Just a dress." I didn't add, "For Dad's wedding," but somehow the words were there and my mother knew. I could tell she knew.

We rode along in silence for several minutes until I finally got the courage to look at her. She glanced back at me and smiled. "Let's get you a dress you'll feel fabulous in."

We didn't go shopping often, and never just the two of us on our own, so at first I felt sort of shy, which is a weird feeling to have with your mom. We usually had Claude either singing or crying and Patrick sulking and trying to look like he wasn't with us. With just us two, there was a lot of silence.

To get to the center of the mall we had to pass all the makeup counters. When I saw a sign that said, "Free Gift with Purchase," I pointed it out.

"Look, Mom. If you buy one thing you get that little carrying case with all those other things in it." My mom doesn't really wear makeup, but they were so pretty, those little pots of color, and my mom was wearing a special blouse and skirt. Maybe it was because she suddenly seemed like a person to me and not just a mom. Maybe I just wanted her to have something nice and new.

"I don't need anything here," Mom said.

I tugged on her arm. "See—there are two different lipsticks and a little square container with four different colors for your eyes, plus some cream for your skin and that tiny bottle of perfume. Look—and it's free. And the carrying case, too. You just have to buy one thing."

"Well—" Mom hesitated in front of the glass display. "What would I buy?"

"Ask the lady," I said. "Excuse me!" I waved my arm to get attention.

The lady behind the counter was wearing a white coat, like a doctor. Her lips were shiny red. She said, "Can I help you?"

"We want the free gift," I said. "For my mom."

"I don't really need anything," Mom said. But she glanced at the woman behind the counter and added, "Well, maybe I do. What do you think?"

The lady tilted her head and squinted at my mom's

face. Then she told Mom that her skin was beautiful—maybe she just needed a little this or that to even out the tone. "May I?" she asked, holding up a small bottle of thick, brown-colored liquid.

Mom nodded.

The lady poured the goopy stuff from the bottle onto a little sponge and patted it all over Mom's face, like a smooth coat of paint. "Yes, that's great," she said, and handed Mom a mirror.

Mom stared into the mirror and turned her face from one side to the other. "Okay," she said suddenly. "I'll buy it." Then she hummed while the lady took her money. I was pretty sure my mother had looked better before she got the goop on, but I didn't tell her that. I just felt happy that she had bought something for herself.

Makeup bag in hand, we made our way to the food court, my mom still humming. I ordered vegetable chow mein while my mom got herself a taco salad. Every once in a while we said something out loud, but mostly we just sat at the little table surrounded by other little tables and watched people eat. The silence didn't feel weird anymore, though.

"This is nice," Mom said. "We never go out like this."

"Yeah," I said.

"Where do you want to look for a dress?"

I finished off the last bite of noodles and pointed across the mall. From the ads I'd seen, it was the store that would offer the most variety.

We rode the escalator up to the second floor. My mother went straight to the pretty dress racks and started the serious business of shuffling through them. "What about this one?" she asked, pulling out a pretty silk dress in cornflower blue. I knew it was cornflower blue because the tag said so.

"No," I said.

"You should at least try it on. The color would be beautiful on you."

"No," I said again. I saw a gray-haired saleslady heading our way. Even before she reached us she was calling out, "Can I help you ladies find something?"

"We're looking for a dress for my daughter," my mother said. "A nice dress." The saleslady looked me up and down—my eyes, my hair, my waist, my arms, and even my chest, which made me squirm and turn away. The two of them hunkered down over the racks of silky fabrics. I said, "I'll just go look over there." I don't think my mom even noticed I was gone.

At the far side of the store, the TV monitors flashed music videos. Wandering up and down among the racks, I suddenly wondered if I would be able to find what I needed.

And even if I did, would I be able to pull it off without my mother seeing me?

It was just at that moment, that sinking-feeling moment, when the most magical thing happened. A salesgirl appeared, but she wasn't like the lady helping my mother. This salesgirl was young, like she might be in high school. She had thick black eyeliner and a skull tattoo on the side of her neck.

"Can I help you find something?" she asked. My own twisted fairy godmother.

I quickly told her what I was looking for, then added, "And I need to keep it hidden from my mom. She's over there." I pointed to the pretty dress section.

The girl laughed. "Got it. No problem. Follow me." She zigzagged through stuffed racks of clothing to the far corner of the store. "I saw this today and thought it was amazing."

As she spoke, she pulled out the most unbelievable dress I had ever seen. It was made of stretchy material, short and clingy, in black and green camouflage print. Around the bottom was all this thick black lace that looked exactly like spiderwebs, and everywhere were these skulls and crossbones, stamped in like angry graffiti. I grabbed it from her and read the label: LOOKS CAN KILL. It was so perfect I couldn't speak.

"Well?"

I nodded gratefully.

"I know. It's like for some end-of-the-world prom. Do you want to try it on?"

"No," I said. "I don't have time. I just need to buy it before my mom sees it."

"Understood," the girl said. "Anyway, I'm sure it will fit you. It looks like your size and it's stretchy material."

She pulled me to the counter and, with lightning speed, rang up the dress. I pulled out my wad of money and placed seven, five-dollar bills on the counter. The girl swept it up and gave me three dollars and a few cents in change. Not bad.

"Do you want it on a hanger?" she asked.

I held up my backpack. "I'll just stuff it in here. And thank you. From the bottom of my heart."

The girl smiled and her black-rimmed eyes sparkled into my own. "Have fun wearing it," she said. "You'll look amazing."

As I wandered back to where I'd left my mom, I looked at the racks of pretty dresses. The colors were so perfect, all Easter egg and seaside taffy. I tried not to think about the silvery-green one in the closet at my dad's house—how it felt when it swirled against my legs.

Stop it, I said to myself. *Stop it, Melissa.*

Silently, my mother appeared at my shoulder, making

me jump. Along with her little bag of makeup, she was now carrying a long plastic bag with the hooked part of a hanger poking out. She kissed me on the top of my head. "Did you find anything to try on?"

I shook my head. "What's in your bag?"

"Oh, just something I found over there." She motioned to the grown-up section. "Something I liked for myself. But we have a whole dressing room started for you."

"I didn't really like anything here," I said.

"Well, let's try another store."

"Actually, Mom, I'm pretty tired."

"Shall we just go home then? There's still some pie left in the fridge. I hid it from Claude."

"There is?" I was surprised. Cherry pie had seemed like years ago. "Yes," I said, suddenly exhausted and wanting pie. "Let's go home."

CHAPTER 29

MAYBE BECAUSE OF MY DREAMS THAT NIGHT—dreams involving skulls and crossbones and spiderweb lace—I woke up groggy the next morning. I was so tired I even pulled the covers over my head to keep out the glowing sunrise. But when Patrick stuck his head into my room and called, "Time to get up, Missy," I remembered my new job in the Little Field. I scrambled out of bed and was ready in record time.

"Bye," I said to my mom as I climbed out of the car. "Bye," I said to Claude.

Claude lunged forward, grabbed my shirt and held on tight. "Stay, Missy. Play!"

"I have to go, Claude."

Mom said, "Claude, Missy is a big girl. She needs to do big girl work. Let go of her now." Which is when he started to cry. Even as they pulled away, I could still hear him crying.

When Mom's car was back on the main road, Patrick hesitated by the garage. He opened his mouth to say something, but then shook his head. "Bye, Missy," he said. And then, "Melissa."

"Bye, Patrick." I opened the garage door and turned on all the lights. There were berries stacked for sorting so I turned on the machine and started in. It didn't feel right to go to the Little Field on my own. It felt too private, like I was walking into their very house. Also, I had the feeling that I should wait until all the kids had been dropped off. That way, no one would be suspicious. No one would come snooping around.

Finally drop-offs were over and I'd sorted all the berries. I turned off the machine. "Bev?" I called in the stillness.

No answer.

I was worried they had forgotten about me. I was worried that I hadn't done a good enough job, or that it had been a big mistake. I walked over to the side door, the one that opened straight into their kitchen. I knocked quietly and waited. A moment later, the door opened.

"Can you find your way on your own?" Bev asked.

I nodded happily.

Being back in the Little Field was as perfect as I'd remembered. The berries were perfect. The sky was perfect. The warm, sandy soil was perfect. But the thing most perfect was the way it made me feel. Moose and Bev trusted me—only me—with their precious field of berries. It was like when Claude had a nightmare and came to me instead of Mom or Dad. Like I was that important.

And every day I loved it more.

There was only one thing that wasn't completely perfect, a certain kind of loneliness, the kind that grew worse when the voices on the other side of the hedge got too close. When I heard those familiar voices from the big field, yelling out a joke or calling for the time, I imagined Patrick and Shauna, standing close and laughing together. Discovering bird nests and secret hiding places and raccoons. Searching for Moose's secret.

But then, a funny thing started to happen. Two funny things. The first was this: Maybe it was being so alone with so much quiet, but those little bushes came to be like friends. It made me think of that rainy day in the big field, when I first heard the plants talk. I was hearing them again, but more often and more distinctly.

The other was that I started seeing things. If I looked

up quickly, I'd often see bright patches of light dancing right above my head. I knew people would call these sunspots or mirages, but I started telling myself they were friendly fairies, coming out to keep me company. Sometimes I talked to them, just to pass the time.

I guess there was a third surprising thing, and that was Moose. Even though Bev had told me that he used only about seven words a day, I found that not to be true. Every time he stopped by to drop off my lunch, or to swap my full buckets for empty ones, we talked. We talked about things like telling time from the sun and about my mom's favorite Western movies. We talked about the odd jobs he and Bev did during the winter months, about the honeybee population, and the surprising varieties of beetles I'd seen in the field. Sometimes, just for fun, I counted up how many words he was using.

So when Moose showed up to surprise me with a late-morning Popsicle, lime green and dripping just as soon as I peeled it out of its white paper, I didn't feel strange blurting out the question, "Moose, do you think plants can talk?"

He smiled and the creases at the corners of his eyes stretched into deep lines. "I thought they only spoke to me."

"No, really," I said.

"Really," Moose answered. "I'm not kidding you.

Why wouldn't they talk? They're alive, aren't they?"

"I thought I was just losing my mind."

"You're not losing your mind."

"Well," I said. "That's good. And what about seeing things? You know, like out of the corner of your eye? Like little flashes of light?"

"That I wouldn't know about," he said. "Bev talks about seeing things sometimes. You can ask her. But the sun can play tricks on your eyes. I recommend you start wearing a hat." And for emphasis, he tipped the worn and dirty brim of his green cap.

We were quiet for a moment when, all of a sudden, the air was filled with such a symphony of buzzing and chirping and rustling that it was almost too loud to bear. Then, just as quickly, it was gone. Moose cleared his throat. "So, tell me. What are they saying to you? The bushes?"

I took my time with the answer. It wasn't so easy to put into words. "Well, they don't say things like sentences, really. More like feelings." I shook my head. "I can't explain it very well."

Moose nodded. "Not everyone has the ability or the desire to be quiet in nature. But if everyone did, well, the world would be a different place."

I licked off the sticky green trail of Popsicle juice

that had slid down my arm and thought of all the other things I wanted to ask him. Like were the people in France enjoying their berries? How about the millionaire in Kentucky? Did he and his brother ever run into each other? Had Al's hands always been so big, or did that just happen with age? But the longer we stood in the silence, the nicer it felt. As I looked across the field to the special little bushes, there was suddenly only one thing I wanted to know.

"Moose," I asked, "why aren't there more bushes like these? You know, with them being so valuable?"

"Well, there are many varieties of blueberries in the world. And all plants that get cultivated for farming have an interesting history. But these, these are personal. Part of their value comes from being unique. These particular bushes," Moose motioned with his arm, "my father developed on his own. He'd work in the field all day, and then at night, he'd go out to his greenhouse and tinker with branches and seeds. Graft this to that."

He shook his head, chuckling. "During the off-season he'd travel around the country, looking at different bushes, different types of soil. That's what we'd do on family vacations, hike around mountains and dig up wild berry bushes. My brother and me, we would ride around in the backseat playing rock, paper, scissors. Anyway, after years of planning and studying and trying things out, he came up with these."

I had been trying to count how many words he was using, but I lost track when he said the word "brother."

"Your brother?" I choked out. My heart was thumping.

Moose nodded.

All the things I'd heard, all the things Shauna and my brother had said, this was my chance to find something out. But how could I bring up a blood feud?

"Then why—"

"I guess I should get back to work," he said stiffly. "Or Bev will send the dogs in after me."

I had done it, broken the magical talking spell.

"Well anyway," I said, "are there really some dogs around here? Because Al has mentioned them."

When Moose laughed, all the stiffness disappeared. "That's just an expression. I don't have dogs anymore. I used to have dogs." He pulled up the sleeve of his farmer shirt and showed me his forearm. "See this?"

I bent down for a closer look. There was a scar. Teeth marks.

"Lyle's dog," Moose explained. "My dogs were never so mean."

It was the first time Moose had ever mentioned his brother by actual name. I jumped at the chance again.

"So Lyle," I started, but I didn't know what to say next.

Moose rolled down his sleeve to cover the mark. "This is from way back. That particular canine is long gone. Anyway, who knows what Lyle is up to these days? He's after these berries. That much I know. And I guess he does have a dog. I hear it barking."

"Why?"

He looked at me, confused. "Why does he have a dog?"

"Why is he after these berries."

"I suppose because he thinks half belong to him."

"Do they?" It was out too quickly, before I could stop it; before I even knew I was going to say it. As my mother would say, "You and your mouth, Missy."

"If they were half his, would they be here in my field?" Moose's voice was still slow like always, but there was something different about it. Something tight and hard that made me wonder.

"No," I said. "Of course not."

I remembered what Bev had said, that they'd once had to secretly move the entire field—all those plants! Had they moved it from Lyle's side? Had they snuck out in the middle of the night and dug up all the precious plants? I imagined it under a full moon.

Right then there was a new silence, not like the nice silence that usually came when Moose was around. This silence brought with it a shadow, even though there wasn't a cloud in the sky. And when the new silence went on long enough to make me squirm, I held up my bare Popsicle stick and said, "Thanks again."

Moose gathered up my full buckets. "Don't mention it. I left extra buckets over there by the shade. I'll bring your lunch out later, right after I make a run with the picking machine." His voice was normal again, but I still felt funny.

After he'd disappeared through the hole in the hedge, I listened for the sounds I'd learned how to hear—the plants, the wind, the grasshoppers, the dirt. But my mind was too loud with questions. I'd been so close to finding out something important, something about Moose and his brother and the giant hedge and the blood feud. And everything he told me just made me wonder more. I bent down over a small bush and tried to find the rhythm, tried to let my fingers take over and do their job.

The pickers on the other side of the hedge seemed to be getting closer. That, or I was just paying more attention. I listened to their songs and the crackle of the radio and how they called out for the time. Their stupid jokes made me laugh, every time, even though they made me feel sad, too. Like I was sitting in that fancy restaurant in France, eating the most amazing meal, all alone.

CHAPTER 30

BY THE TIME MOOSE RETURNED WITH LUNCH, MY T-shirt was drenched. Sweat dripped down my forehead and stung my eyes. "Someone turned up the dial on summer," Moose said.

"I wish they'd turn it down."

"You come in if it starts to get to you. Don't want a case of the heat stroke on our hands." Along with my lunch sack, Moose held out a can of soda. "From Bev."

"Tell her thanks." I stood right there, popped the tab, and took a long, cold drink. All the weirdness of earlier appeared to be gone, but, inside, my head was starting to buzz. Maybe this was it—another chance to find out about the mysterious blood feud.

Moose picked up my little bucket and started to pick. His boots sunk in the sandy soil. "My daddy used to help me pick sometimes. He had big strong hands, and my bucket filled up so fast when he did. Like magic."

I tried to imagine the farm way back when Moose was a boy, before parts were sold off and the rest sliced down the middle. I kept my voice casual when I asked, "Did he help Lyle, too?"

"Oh, sure. He never played favorites."

If he hadn't played favorites, then why did Moose end up with the most valuable part of the field? I bit my lip so I wouldn't say what I was thinking. *Stop your mouth, Missy,* but it was too late because next thing that happened, I heard my own voice blabbing. "Well, then, how is it that you got this Little Field? Why does it all belong to you and not Lyle, too?"

Moose didn't answer for a long time, and I was pretty sure I'd blown it. But then, in a quiet and calm voice he said, "My father wanted things to stay the way they were. He made us promise certain things about how the field would be run. I respected that and my brother didn't."

"So—" *Careful, Missy. Careful.* "Your father gave it to you because you made the promise?"

"My brother made the promise, too. But then he went back on that promise."

"So originally, your dad left it to you both?" I was pressing, in my very Missy way, but I couldn't stop. As Patrick always says, it's my very worst quality.

"He left everything to us to run together. He never wanted to see it split up."

"And your brother—"

"He was off seeing the world. Having adventures." Moose was still looking down, still picking, so I couldn't see his eyes. After a moment he added, "My father had a certain way of doing things, running his farm with a certain order." He straightened up. When he handed back my little bucket it was piled high. "You have both your parents still?"

"What?" The question startled me. *Did I have both my parents?*

"Are both your parents alive?"

"They're alive," I said. "Sure."

"Well, my father is no longer with us, you see. This year, I'm turning the same age he was when he died. That's why I wanted kids out again, in his field. Real pickers, not just machines that tear the place apart. I wanted to hear voices again, and radios playing music. Doing things his way, well, it's my way of paying respect to him. Every day I get to say, 'Hello, Daddy—I'm taking care of your things.' That's about all I have left anymore. It's what I wanted to do for him this year. That's all."

There was something in his face right then that was too open, too exposed. It made me want to slink away, unnoticed. Like when you catch a glimpse of someone praying when they think they're all alone. His hawk-eyes had softened, leaving deep, sagging creases in the corners. Deep creases and a secret sadness. I hadn't counted words, but I knew those were the most real ones anyone had ever said to me.

At the time, I didn't know what a treasure it was, being handed words like that. But I did know it was something. Something to care for. Something to protect. I thought, *Maybe that's all I'll ever know about the secrets of blueberries. Maybe that is enough.*

The rest of the day flew by. When the sun was nearly at its three o'clock spot and I was gathering my things to go, I heard them. Directly on the other side of the hedge. Footsteps and rustling bushes. Whispers. A radio turned low.

I froze.

Someone called out for the time, in that funny way that made it sound like a joke. It could have been one of those Smith brothers Shauna was always talking about.

"Shut up!" hissed another voice, one I didn't recognize, practically in my ear. "We're not supposed to be over this far!"

The first voice called out again anyway. "What–time–is–it?"

And then came the answers, echoing from different corners of the big field. Some of them were close. Too close.

"Same time it was yesterday at this time!"

"Time for you to shut your mouth!"

"Time for you to get a watch!"

I'd heard it all before, but it all still made me smile.

"Seriously," he called again. "What time is it for real?"

And that's when another voice shouted back, loud and clear. "It's a quarter to—the monkey's poo!"

Laughter erupted from all sides of the field. I couldn't help it—I laughed, too. All the way along the path to the house I giggled at that new answer.

Back in the coolness of the garage, Bev handed me a crisp, new twenty-dollar bill. "That's just a bonus, hon," she said. "For all your hard work."

I thought about telling them, about the voices on the other side of the hedge being so close, but I stopped myself. I was afraid they would pull me from the Little Field and I'd have to go back to sorting berries. Anyway, I told myself, I would be able to keep watch out there. I'd be helping them by staying.

When Moose handed me a brown paper sack, I didn't have to peek to know what was inside.

CHAPTER 31

DRIVING HOME, PATRICK ASKED MOM IF SHE WOULD take him to the lake. "Now?" she asked.

"Well, I need to get my suit and towel first. But, yeah, a bunch of kids are going. If you drop me off, I can probably get a ride home."

Mom thought about it for a minute. "Okay," she said, and told him to be home by dinnertime. "You too, Missy?" she asked.

From my spot in the backseat I studied my big brother's face, the way his jaw got stiff at the mention of me coming along. So I said, "Maybe," just to watch his jaw get even tighter.

Claude reached over and tried to grab the paper bag

from me, the one with the berries from the Little Field. I leaned close to his ear and whispered, "We'll have them later, okay, Mr. Claudio?" He sucked on his fingers, thinking this over. Finally he nodded.

"The lake used to seem so far away," I said loudly. No one answered so I added, "When we used to go out there as a family." No one answered again.

Mom asked me to stay with Claude while she drove Patrick. As soon as the front door shut, Claude pestered me for the blueberries again. "Big boo-berries, Missy!"

I took the paper bag to the kitchen and tucked them in a corner of the pantry. "Bad Missy!" He charged after me like a little bull. "Bad!"

I tried not to laugh. "They're for later, Claude," I said. "I promise. Let's do something special now. Something really fun."

I led him to our room and crawled underneath my bed. Digging through my Intruder objects, I finally found all the pieces to my old castle set—the walls and furniture, knights and dragons, horses and princesses. I tossed them out, piece by piece, and heard Claude's happy squeal with each new treasure. When I was done, he shoved his big head underneath the bed. "No more, Claude," I said. I rolled out and brushed the dust from my shirt. "Let's play."

I set up in the middle of the room. First, I organized all my big pieces. Then I connected the base for the castle, stacked up the walls, and added the windows and the drawbridge. Claude picked up the prettiest horse and smashed it against the tower.

I pointed to the fake water that circled the castle. It had always been my favorite feature. "That's the moat," I told him. "There are alligators in it. Be careful or they will eat your horse." Claude shrieked with delight.

I imagined Patrick at the lake in his new swimsuit. I imagined Shauna, too. Talking and laughing and swimming out to the floating dock.

The lake used to be my favorite place, back when I was a little kid. It had seemed so far away, like it was a big adventure to get there. Even though it was a state park and had an official name, we just called it Deep Lake.

Deep Lake had everything: a campsite, and a dock for fishing, and boats you could rent, and two different swimming areas, one on either side. On perfect summer nights, my parents would pack up hot dogs and buns and a can of Boston baked beans and also a package of marshmallows, and then we'd drive out to the lake.

It was just the four of us then, Mom and Dad and me and Patrick. We'd go as soon as Mom and Dad got home from work, and while other families would pitch tents and spend the weekend, we called what we did Friday Evening Campout.

At the far side swimming area, near the campground, we'd find an empty fire pit to set up camp. First, though, we'd leave our bundle of wood and our cooler of food and head straight to the lake to swim. When the sun went down, we'd dry off quickly and run back to our camp. While Dad started the fire, Patrick and I searched the woods until we found four perfect sticks for roasting hot dogs and marshmallows. Mom warmed up the beans in a camp pot that was blackened on the bottom. We'd tell stories and eat more marshmallows in front of the fire until I got sleepy. Then, in the dark, we'd load the car and drive slowly away, past the glowing patches of light from other campsites.

As I looked at Claude, battling a fairy princess against my favorite knight, I felt sad for him, sad that he'd never had a Friday Evening Campout with both Mom and Dad. But I guess that meant he wouldn't miss it like I did.

"Play, Missy!" he shouted in my face.

I picked up another knight and placed it on my favorite horse. I galloped it around the castle shouting, "I will get you and eat you up!" Claude laughed so hard he fell over on his side.

Even though I was having fun with Claude, I couldn't

stop thinking about Patrick. I wondered what he was doing at that very moment. I imagined him on the other side of the lake, the one without campsites. My dad had taken us there when we wanted to go fishing, because you could fish off a long wooden dock. It was the side you could also rent rowboats and buy other things in the store that smelled like lake water, things like sunscreen and potato chips and worms for fishing. Lake water is the best smell there is.

Also on that side was a swimming dock. It's where the older kids swam because there was a lifeguard on duty, sitting in a tall chair, and a diving board off the dock, and also a floating dock, way out that you could swim to.

The summer before, I'd gone to the lake with Constance and Allie. The rule was we had to stay in the lifeguard area. I showed them all the great things, like where to fish and buy worms. Just as long as I didn't look across to the other side, where the campsites and all my family memories were, I could have an okay time.

Patrick went once last summer, on his own, and then not again. He had Dad drop him off in the morning and pick him up in the afternoon. When he got back his face was red, but not sunburned, and he went straight to his room. I followed him. That's when he told me they had called him Praying Mantis Boy.

"Who did?"

"My friends."

"Those aren't friends if they'd do that," I said to him.

"Oh, Missy." His voice was like Mom's when she got tired of trying to explain something. He didn't say anything else, so after a while I stopped asking him questions and just tiptoed out of his room. We never talked about it again.

I wondered if his new fancy swimsuit would make any difference. I wondered if he would look across the lake to the campground side, and remember our Friday Night Campouts. I wondered if he missed them as much as I did.

Claude's horse was being eaten by an alligator. Just as my knight jumped in to save it, I heard the front door close. "Mom?" I called.

She came and stood in the doorway. "How's Mr. Claude?" she asked.

"We're playing with my old castle. How's Patrick?"

Mom smiled. "He met up with his friends. He's getting a ride home later. Will you help me with dinner? Just peel some carrots? I just need fifteen more minutes to finish up my work for the day."

I told Claude we'd finish playing castle in the kitchen. I set up a chair next to the sink and while I peeled carrots,

Claude stood on the chair and dunked his horses in the water. He draped his knights with long, thin carrot peels. "Play, Missy," he said.

But I couldn't even pretend to play anymore. All I could think about was Patrick, his new friends, and all the fun he was having at the lake.

CHAPTER 32

THAT NIGHT AT DINNER, PATRICK TOLD FUNNY STORIES about the lake. He told about Giant Johnny and the Smith brothers and how some guy they called Earlobe found a dead fish. Claude laughed so hard food flew out of his mouth.

"Do you know these kids, too?" Mom asked, turning to me. "With all their strange names?"

I shook my head. "I'm too busy working. And besides, I don't see what's so funny about throwing a dead fish around."

While Patrick cleared the dinner dishes, I made a loud announcement. "Everyone sit! Get ready for a surprise dessert!" Then I went to the cupboard where my mom kept her special things. I had to stand on a chair and on my tiptoes to reach what I was looking for—the set of delicate crystal bowls, a wedding present for my parents, way back when. We hadn't used them since Dad moved out.

One by one, I took out four bowls from the darkest corner of the cupboard and lined them on the kitchen counter. Then I took Moose's brown paper bag and carefully divided up the Little Field berries.

"Ta-da," I called, walking to the table with a bowl in each hand.

"Ta-da," I said again as I set the two bowls on the table, one in front of Claude and one in front of Mom. Claude clapped his hands. He knew all about these berries. Mom and Patrick just stared.

I spun around, back to the kitchen, and grabbed the other two bowls. "For you," I said to Patrick, setting down the bowl but avoiding his eyes. Claude had waited, just like a grown-up little man. The beauty of the bowls must have brought out something in him; some sort of signal that this moment was special.

Patrick looked from the bowl to my face, then back to the bowl. He picked up a berry and examined it closely. "Where did you get these, Missy?"

"Where do you think? Moose gave them to me after I was done sorting."

Patrick shook his head. "These aren't regular berries. There are no berries like this in our field."

"Of course there are. Where else would Moose have gotten them?" I glanced over at Mom and saw that she was too busy staring at the crystal bowls to notice the berries, or our conversation.

"I hope you don't mind I got out the bowls, Mom. I should have asked first."

She looked up at me, shaking her head. Her eyes filled with tears.

"Oh, Mom. I'm sorry–"

"No, Missy," she said quickly. "It's okay. It's *good*. They are such beautiful bowls and they belong to our family. We should eat out of them. We should always remember to enjoy beautiful things together."

"Thanks, Mom."

Mom cleared her throat and smiled. She picked up her first berry. When she popped it in her mouth, her eyes opened wide. "My goodness," she said. "I've never tasted a blueberry like this before."

Patrick continued to stare at me. "So, Moose gave them to you?"

"Yes."

"But do you know where he got them?"

"I told you. His field. Where else?"

"Right," he said. And at that moment, I had exactly what I'd wanted.

Later, while Mom was giving Claude his bath, Patrick and I stood at the sink, hand washing the crystal bowls. "So how was the lake?" I asked him.

"Fine," he said.

"Did you go off the diving board?"

"A few times."

"Swim out to the dock?"

"Yeah."

"Who drove you home?"

"Shauna's mom." He handed me a clean bowl to dry. When I turned it in my hand, it sparkled like it was filled with a hundred little lights. "Missy," he said quietly, "where do you go during the day?"

"What?" My hand froze on the bowl.

"When you say you're working in the sorting garage, where are you really?"

"I'm in the sorting garage."

"No you're not."

"How do you know?"

"I just know."

"But how do you know?" I carefully set the dry bowl on the counter and waited for the next one. My heart was beating a warning signal. *Da-bump. Da-bump.*

Patrick said, "Shauna went up there today and you weren't there."

"Maybe I was going to the bathroom."

"She waited."

"What?"

"She watched and waited. She said you weren't there. She waited for an hour."

I tried to make sense of what he was telling me. "You're spying on me?"

"No. We just need to find out about something."

"What?" I demanded. "What do you need to find out?"

"Well, we all thought since you were up in the sorting garage you might have heard something useful."

"What do you mean by *we all*?"

"What?"

"You said *we all*."

"Missy, listen. There are some things you should know about Moose." He handed me another bowl. "Come out with me tomorrow. Come out and meet the other kids. You'll like them. I know you will."

"But what do they want from Moose?"

"They just want to find something. A long time ago Moose stole something from Lyle. But Lyle can't come onto his field to get it back."

"How do you know all this? How do you know anything about Lyle?"

"Some of the kids, their parents worked in the fields years ago. They remember what happened. They knew Lyle really well. So we went over there. To meet him."

"You crossed over? To the other side of the hedge?"

"We did, Missy. I told you we found an opening. Close your mouth."

I couldn't close my mouth. It felt permanently open in a shocked way.

"Missy, really. Lyle's a nice guy. He uses picking machines but said we could even pick for him, if we wanted. He said he'd pay us more than Moose."

"What do you know about anything?"

"I know that Moose is a thief. And a liar. I didn't know for sure until you brought those berries home. Now I know. I know what people are saying is true. About the Little Field."

My stomach twisted. He wasn't supposed to know. No one was supposed to know anything about it. "Well," I said slowly. "I don't know anything. Like I said. Moose just handed them to me in a brown paper sack. Are you done washing that yet?"

Patrick looked down at the sudsy water. "But Shauna said—"

"Who are you going to believe? Me or Shauna?" I grabbed the crystal bowl from him and rubbed it dry. "Are we done?"

He looked in the water. "Yeah," he said. "But, Missy—"

"I'm going to bed," I said.

Later, I would think about that night and how it started something in motion. Or maybe it was all in motion anyway, and I just turned it up a notch. I do know this: If I'd thought it through, all the way to the very end, I wouldn't have done it. I would have kept those Little Field berries a secret, like I knew I was supposed to.

CHAPTER 33

IT WAS THE DAY THAT WOULD END UP BEING NOT ONLY the hottest of the summer, but also the hottest in the entire recorded history of our town. Maybe it was the heat that did it, made everyone do things they wouldn't ordinarily do. I've heard that heat can do that to people. I know I didn't sleep much the night before the hottest day, and part of it was the twisting around in sweaty sheets. The other part, though, was that my head was spinning from what Patrick had told me. He had gone to the other side of the hedge! He had met Lyle! He was calling Moose a thief! And a liar!

With too many thoughts and very little sleep, I didn't feel so good when I walked into the kitchen that next morning. Patrick was there already, slapping meat onto a slice of bread.

"Good morning," I said fake brightly. I pushed the button on Mom's Mr. Coffee and looked around for something else to do so I wouldn't have to look at him.

"Okay, Missy. I mean it. Tell me where you got those berries."

"I told you already."

"You lied. I *know* you're not in the sorting garage when you say you are. I *know* you came home with berries that look like they're from another planet. I *know* there's a field of berries that Moose is hiding from Lyle. So tell the truth."

"It sounds like you know everything already. Why bother asking me?"

He clenched his jaw. "Missy—"

Right then Claude stomped into the kitchen with a doll stuffed underneath his pajama top. "My baby!" he shouted, patting the bump.

"You have a baby, Mr. Claudio?" I turned all my attention on him. I bent down and poked his tummy. He laughed.

Patrick chopped my sandwich in half, the wrong way. "You are such a liar." He stuffed it into a sandwich bag. "Do you want an apple or a banana?"

"Apple." I stayed where I was, on the floor with

Claude, to hide my face. I tickled him. I made a funny blowing noise on his cheek. He giggled and squirmed, karate chopped my head, and bit my thumb.

"No biting, Claude," I said sternly, while trying not to laugh at his strange mix of person and animal.

"More boo-berries," he demanded. "More big boo-berries."

I looked up at Patrick. "Why do you even care? Why do you care so much?"

"I told you everything, Missy. I tried to include you. And you—you knew something all along. You've been keeping it from me."

"You never included me! You said I was too hard to be around!"

"Well, when you wear those stupid glasses—"

"It was before that, Patrick."

"Missy, I like someone. And she likes me."

I stood up, grabbed two apples from the bowl on the counter, held them to my chest and marched around. "I'm Shauna," I said in a high-pitched voice. Claude laughed and reached for an apple, too. The doll slipped from underneath his shirt.

"More BOO-BERRIES," he shouted.

"Listen, Missy." Patrick's voice was serious. "Tell me now. If you don't, I'll tell Mom what I know."

"What do you know?"

"That you're not where you're supposed to be."

I was so mad I could barely get the words out. "I'm not the one who disappeared in the field. I'm not the one who left you all alone, out in the rain. You tell Mom on me and guess what? I tell on you!" I slammed the apples back onto the counter.

Claude picked up the doll and swung it at my legs. That's when Mom walked into the kitchen, her hair uncombed and her eyes puffy from sleep. She went straight to the cupboard for her favorite mug. "What are you two arguing about this time?"

We glanced at each other but stayed silent. Mom poured cream in her coffee and took her first sip of the day. "Ahh," she said. "My clock stopped working in the night. What time is it anyway?"

It came out before I could stop it.

It came out without me telling it to.

It came out completely on its own.

"It's a quarter to the monkey's poo—" and then I slapped my hand to my mouth because I realized.

Patrick's butter knife froze in midair. His eyes quickly shifted to my face. "Wait. What did you say?"

"Nothing." I picked up Claude and danced him around the kitchen. "Nothing."

"You said monkey poo—"

"That's what I thought," Mom said. "Why did you say that?"

"Monkey POO!" Claude yelled gleefully. "Monkey POO!"

"It was something someone said in the field yesterday, Mom," Patrick explained slowly. "It was a new joke. Smith Three called it out. But, Missy, I'm surprised you heard it all the way from the sorting garage. You can't really hear anything from up there, can you?"

My cheeks were burning so I kept my face down and continued to waltz with Claude.

"Smith Three." Mom shook her head. "What do they call you, Patrick?"

"Just 'Patrick,' Mom," he said. "But, Missy, I'm serious. How did you hear it?"

My left eye began to twitch, and I wondered what would seem more truthful: to meet Patrick's gaze or keep my eyes hidden?

"Missy is a monkey POO!" Claude shrieked. He was hysterical, with drool rolling down his cheek. "Monkey POO!"

"That's not nice, Claude," Mom said. She grabbed her keys from the counter. "Let's go to the car."

I held Claude like a shield. "I'll carry him out, Mom.

We're having fun." Claude howled and tried to squirm out of my arms, but I held on tight. He bit my arm. "Claude! I told you. No biting!"

Mom wrestled Claude away from me and set him firmly on the ground.

"Monkey POO!" he yelled at her. "You are a monkey POO!"

Mom shot her laser eyes across the kitchen. First they burned straight into me and then into Patrick. "I don't know what's going on with you two," she said quietly, "but stop it. Finish up the lunches and meet me in the car." As she started out the kitchen with the howling Claude, I tried to follow.

"Hold on one second, Missy." Patrick stepped out, blocking my way. When we heard the front door close he said, "You heard the joke."

"So?"

"So, you heard it from the Little Field."

"I heard it from the sorting garage. Let's go."

"That means it's close by. And somewhere near the garage, too."

"I have no idea what you're talking about. Mom's waiting."

"You know exactly what I'm talking about. Why are you doing this?"

"Doing what?"

"I thought we were together. I thought we were a team."

"That's what I thought, too. Until—until—"

"What?"

"Until you started acting so stupid! Like such a joke! Like such a stupid, skinny, ridiculous joke!" The minute the words were out I wished I could take them back. They were terrible words, words I didn't mean at all. Words that were meant to hurt because I was hurt. They were the kind of words that could maybe start a blood feud.

Patrick stared at me, like he was looking at a stranger, not a sister. But as he turned and headed for the door, I noticed a funny smile at the corner of his mouth. I remember thinking, "Well, he's smiling. Everything must be okay, after all."

But later I would think back to that moment and know. I'd know exactly what a smile like that really meant.

CHAPTER 34

THAT MORNING I PICKED FASTER THAN EVER. WHEN Moose didn't show up by the time I'd filled both big buckets and my little one, too, I decided to walk them back to the sorting garage myself.

The hidden trail seemed longer than usual. The buckets felt extra heavy, and the sun was already too hot on my head. At the back porch, I set down my buckets and grabbed the knob to the garage door. It was locked.

"Bev? Moose?" I knocked and called again. "Bev? Are you in there?" A moment later I heard footsteps, then the door opened and Bev peeked out.

"You're fast today," she said, opening it wide. "Sorry

about the door. I never showed you the button to push to make sure it's unlocked."

"That's okay." I picked up my buckets and stepped inside.

"It's a hot one already. Moose is still out with the truck."

I glanced past the open garage doors at the gravel drive. I wondered if I should say something to Bev about the slip-up with my brother. I took a deep breath and started, but the words just wouldn't come out. She would only be mad at me and I didn't think I could stand that— having her mad at me, too.

As I turned away from the open doors, though, I saw a flash of something, all the way across the gravel, over by the hedge. I looked back at the spot, just past our overturned buckets.

"What's the matter, hon?" Bev asked. "You look jumpy." She came and stood right next to me and squinted out across the gravel drive. "Do you see something?"

"No," I said. "Maybe." I held my breath, waiting for it to reappear. I thought about Shauna, spying on me. I shivered. "For a minute I thought I saw something," I said. "Like a flash of white."

Bev put her hand on my shoulder. "Maybe you've been out in the sun too long. Let me see your eyes."

I turned to her and looked in her face. "Aha," she said. "Just as I thought. You're suffering from lack of break time with me."

I laughed. "Yeah, maybe."

She stepped into the kitchen and came out with two cold sodas. We crunched across the gravel drive and settled down on our overturned buckets. I started to feel a little bit better. The sun was shining; the sky was about as blue as blue could be; and nothing bad could happen to me. I took a sip of soda.

"I see things sometimes," Bev said. "Out of the corner of my eye."

"When the sun is too bright?"

"No. More like when I look up quickly. I see shadows. Shapes."

"Really?"

She looked at me. "Do you see them, too?"

"Moose said they were from the sun. But I pretend they are little fairies. Out to keep me company."

Bev said quietly, "I see two dancing boys. That's what I turn them into. It helps me think of happier times." Then she shook her head and laughed.

"What do you mean happier times?"

"Oh, just Moose and his brother," she said, staring across the drive. "My goodness it's hot!"

I remembered what Moose said about their family

vacations, sitting in the backseat playing rock, paper, scissors. I tried to picture Moose as a boy.

"So what happened to them? Why did they divide the farm? Why did they plant the hedge?" My brother's words were like a plant in my brain, growing wild with twisting roots.

Bev shook her head. "How about we save it for another day?"

"Okay," I said. Then I thanked her for the soda and told her I should be getting back out there.

"Remind me to get a hat for you," she said, crumpling her can. "So you don't start seeing my little mirages along with your own."

I thought about what Moose had said, about my talking plants. "Maybe there is magic around us. Maybe we just need time and quiet to see it all clearly."

She smiled straight into my eyes. "That's a nice thought, Melissa."

Suddenly, more than anything, I wanted her to know my real name. "Bev?"

"Hmm?"

But when I opened my mouth, it was too much. It was too hot, and my head was too full of the crazy confusion of the night before, and the morning, and the terrible words I'd said to my brother. So I just said, "Nothing." I couldn't stay there to say one more thing.

CHAPTER 35

BACK IN THE LITTLE FIELD I WAS NERVOUS AND JITTERY. I told myself it was from the soda, and I forced my hands to work fast so I wouldn't have to think. When the sun got so hot on the top of my head that it almost hurt, I suddenly remembered the hat. Bev had forgotten to give me a hat.

The sun said noon when my two big buckets were full again, and still there was no sign of Moose. When I straightened quickly, lights flickered in front of my eyes, but I blinked hard and they went away.

I unhooked my little bucket and walked across the hot, sandy soil toward the shady strip near the hedge. Halfway there I saw something shimmer in the grass. I bent down for a closer look. It was a snakeskin! I'd never seen a snakeskin before. It looked so delicate and thin I was afraid it would crumble when I touched it, but it was surprisingly strong. All my other feelings about the day left me and I was suddenly happy, thinking about taking it home to Claude. Patrick, too. I poured my berries into the big bucket and placed the snakeskin right on top.

My head, where the hair parted down the middle, was burning. I scooted into the shade of the hedge just as much as I could. The air was so hot, it almost hurt to take a breath and I noticed that my arms, already tan to the T-shirt line, were taking on the crispy look of a slow-roasting chicken from the supermarket rotisserie.

Moose had better come soon, I thought to myself, and just as I thought it I heard footsteps from the other side of the hedge. My throat tingled with the thought of a cold soda, or maybe even a Popsicle.

I pulled the 3-D glasses from my back pocket. The plastic border made a tiny bit of shade for my eyes. Then I picked up my snakeskin, all ready to show Moose. I was sure he's seen a million of them, but still, it was something to share. I looked at it again, more closely this time, and could see exactly where the snake used to be—all the little ridges on its underside and even the bulge of the eyes. It was like a ghost of the snake.

I twisted around, impatient for Moose. It seemed

he was taking an extra-long time. "Hello?" I called. "Moose?"

I listened for his footsteps, or the clanging of empty buckets, but there was nothing. Just the bugs and bees sounding louder than usual. I jumped up to look for him, but my head got so dizzy I had to sit back down. Which is when I saw it.

The dog.

At first I thought it was a new mirage—a big white one, out in the middle of the field. But then it began slinking toward me like a hunter would. I couldn't believe it. A dog!

Where did it come from? Was it friendly? I put up my arm, like a crossing guard to an oncoming car. "Stay," I said, my voice loud but shaking. "Sit."

The dog didn't listen but trotted to the edge of the sandy field. He crouched there and made a low, growling sound in his throat. The sound made me afraid.

I glanced over at the opening in the hedge. No sign of Moose, but the slight movement, just the glance, was enough to get the dog back on his feet. He made the noise again and his tail started to wag. Was that a good sign or a bad one? I had no idea. I didn't know anything about dogs, except that they scared me. And that they had teeth that could tear through raw meat.

The dog opened his mouth and barked sharply, showing off pointy white teeth. Slowly I reached over and picked up my empty little bucket. My fingers wrapped around the metal rim and I brought it in front of me, holding it like a shield. I meant it as protection, but it must have looked to the dog like something else. A threat or a toy, I don't know, but it was something that caused the dog to jump and change position, like he was either bowing or getting ready to attack. I didn't wait around to see which one.

Clutching the bucket shield, I made a dash for the hedge opening and squeezed through. Prickles scratched my skin, but I didn't care. I sprinted down the dark pathway, certain that the dog was gaining on me. I could practically feel his breath at my heels, but I didn't look back to see. When I reached the end, I threw myself through the hole in the hedge. I stumbled into the backyard, past the broken barbecue and rusted lawn chair, leaped up on the back porch, and grabbed the doorknob. It was locked.

"Bev!" I shouted, pounding. "Bev! Moose! Bev!"

I turned and pressed my back against the door. The dog was there, panting like crazy, just a few yards away from me. I held up my bucket.

He bent low and growled.

"Bev!" I shouted, kicking at the door. "I'm locked out! Help!"

The dog inched closer, growling still. I threw my bucket, straight at his head, and then turned back to the door. Behind me I heard the clang of the bucket, and then a whimper. Before I could look the door flung opened and Bev stood, spatula in hand. "What the—"

I pushed her back inside yelling, "Dog! Close the door! Dog! Dog!"

"What?"

I slammed the door. "There was a dog—" I panted. "A dog—"

Bev took me by the elbow to the middle of the garage, grabbed a white plastic bucket and turned it over. "You sit here," she said. "I'll call Moose."

I sat on the bucket and tried to breathe. I heard her in the office, making the call. Then I heard her open the back door and say soft words to the dog. My teeth were on the verge of chattering, which didn't make any sense with all the heat. I wondered about the dog. Had I killed it with the bucket?

When Moose finally drove up, his face was all business. Bev met him in the driveway and I heard her say, "I'm pretty sure it's his." They both glanced at me.

I'd finally caught my breath but hadn't managed to

stop the shakes. Moose opened the back door and said some soft words like, "Hey, buddy. Hey, boy." And then the dog came wagging inside, playful and panting.

"Oh," I said. "I thought he was vicious." But I still couldn't stop the shakes. In fact, they'd turned into something else—something like shivering. Along with feeling stupid, I'd wasted good work time. "I'm sorry," I said. "I have two big buckets full of berries still in the field. I'll go get them."

But Bev gave me a look that told me to stay right where I was. "I'll get you something to drink, hon. I have to make a phone call about that dog. Don't worry. He's not going to hurt you."

While Bev made the phone call, Moose rubbed the dog's back. The dog rolled over and stuck his feet in the air, begging Moose to scratch his belly. I noticed his nose was bleeding. "I think I hurt him," I said. "I threw a bucket. I thought he was going to bite me."

"It's just his nose," Moose said. "A tiny cut."

Bev came back to the sorting shed and stood with her hands on her hips until Moose looked up. She nodded her head. "He got loose about an hour ago. They don't know how. But he's coming to fetch him."

Moose nodded slowly. "I think I'll clear out of here until—"

"No you don't, Moose. You stay here and at least face him. At least that."

Moose said, "I've got work to do."

"Just stay." She turned to me. "Do you want a soda, hon?"

I shook my head. "Maybe just some water."

"Okay." But she didn't move.

I'm not sure how long we sat there like that, Moose saying, "I have to get back to work!" and Bev saying, "Stay and face him." Then all at once the puppy gave a happy yelp, scrambled to his feet, and bounded past me. He ran straight through the open garage doors and across the gravel drive. And that's when I heard the voice.

If I hadn't been looking at him right in front of me, I would have sworn the voice belonged to Moose.

When the voice said, "How'd you get loose, anyway?" I knew who it was. I knew exactly who was walking up the gravel drive behind me. All I could think was, this is it. Here it comes. Here comes the blood feud.

CHAPTER 36

"YOUR DOG WAS ON MY PROPERTY." MOOSE'S VOICE WAS
dull and flat and so opposite a blood feud voice that I
nearly fell off the bucket.

"Well, you know animals," said the other voice.
"They don't understand property lines. A hedge is just
a hedge to a dog."

I swiveled around so I could look at that face, and
gasped out loud when I saw it. The man with Moose's
voice—Lyle!—was crouched down and examining his
dog, so I couldn't see exactly what kind of size he was. But
it was his face I couldn't stop staring at. It was Moose's
face, only through one of those mirrors at the carnival,

the kind that changes just a couple of things so you see a slightly warped version of yourself.

Lyle said, "How'd this happen? This cut on his nose?"

"He chased one of my pickers," Moose said.

"I'll have to take him to the vet."

"I'm sorry," I whispered.

Lyle squinted at me, sitting on my white bucket. "So he was all the way down the hill, huh? He chased you all the way back up here?"

I knew exactly what he was getting at. Moose did, too. He stepped in front of me and said, "Your dog was loose on my property. He scared one of my workers. And you happen to be on my property right now, too."

"What's that, big brother?"

The way he said it made me jump. I felt Bev's hand tighten on my shoulder and wondered how long it had been there. "I don't feel too good, Bev," I whispered up to her. "My stomach is kind of queasy."

"You just sit here and rest," she said.

The puppy padded over to me with his head bowed down. Lyle straightened up to a full-size man. "Come, Tippy."

But Tippy didn't listen. He found my hand and nuzzled it, like a big wet apology. I wanted to laugh and cry. I couldn't stop the shivers. "Nice puppy," I said softly. "Nice dog. I'm sorry."

"How's Helen?" Bev asked suddenly. Her voice was tight, like my mom sounded with my dad sometimes.

"She's fine. I know she'd want me to give you her best."

"Back to her," Bev said. After a moment she added, "I miss talking with her." I looked up to her face and saw a heavy sadness. Moose cleared his throat and so did Lyle.

"Well then, sorry about my pup," Lyle said curtly.

"Okay then," Moose answered.

Lyle turned his back to us and whistled for his dog. "Come, Tippy. Come, boy." We all watched Lyle cross the drive and head to the road.

Bev sighed when he was out of sight.

I said, "Could I maybe have some water?"

"Sure," she said. But she didn't move. Not even her eyes. They still looked out, across the drive, to the giant hedge.

Moose, back at his truck, unloaded flats of berries. He worked fast and hard, and whistled a sharp, loud tune.

So this was the blood feud, I thought to myself. I had imagined it as some epic battle with flashing swords and suits of armor. But what I'd seen instead was the complete opposite. Something dark and silent and so dried up and cold that it made my bones hurt.

Moose passed with his crates, and I tried again. "I'm sorry."

He didn't slow down. "What are you sorry about?" As if nothing had happened.

"You know. The dog. I was just sitting there waiting for you. I thought I heard you coming."

"And then it was the dog?"

"Yes," I said. I was piecing it back together. I had found a snakeskin. I was wearing my 3-D glasses. "Well, no. See the dog was in the middle of the field when I looked up."

My head was pounding. I could feel my heartbeat in my ears. "I heard a noise. The next thing I knew there was this dog running at me. I just got so scared. I was thinking about the scar on your arm. The one you showed me that day."

Bev still hadn't moved from her spot next to me, watching the place where Lyle had last been. "I wonder what happened to the last Tippy?" she said, almost to herself.

"What?" I asked.

"He names all his dogs Tippy. The last one was brown and black. It was the name of their childhood dog."

"I didn't know he was just a puppy. I thought he was going to eat me. Maybe, can I have some water, please?"

Bev said, "Sure, hon," but she still didn't move.

Moose came back to the garage, rubbing his head. "So, I'm a little confused. You said you heard footsteps? You thought it was me?"

"I heard footsteps, yes. I thought it was you. Then I saw the dog. Standing in the field." My throat was burning I wanted water so bad.

Moose shook his head. "But you heard footsteps?"

"Well, I heard something. I thought it was you. And then you weren't there."

"So what you heard was the dog?"

"Sure," I said. But as I said it a cold shiver ran up the back of my neck. What I'd heard had made me think Moose was there. So what I'd heard sounded more like a person. Or did I just think it sounded like a person?

The harder I tried to remember, the more I kept picturing something else: my brother's face at the dinner table, holding up one of the berries from the Little Field; my brother's face that morning, hearing me repeat the joke with the monkey poo. All I could see was my brother's face. It was right there, dancing on the edge of my brain—a terrible thought that I couldn't bear to let myself have. And there had been that flash of something near the hedge earlier, too, when I'd come in with my first load of berries. What had I seen? Had someone been hiding, waiting to follow me?

"Moose," I started, getting shakily to my feet. Moose was already out the door.

"You stay here, hon," Bev said.

But I was running past her, out the back door and across the worn and empty yard.

CHAPTER 37

HE WAS STILL AS A STATUE WHEN I GOT THERE. HE WAS crouched over a small bush in the first row. My head was spinning, and my stomach felt like I might get sick. I asked, "What happened?" Even though I knew. Because even before I saw it, I felt it. The tiny bushes had been picked clean. There was not a berry left. I looked out across the field for an actual, physical sign that someone had been there, but except for the footprints, there was nothing. My full buckets were gone, too.

"Did you see anyone, Moose?" I held my breath, waiting.

Moose shook his head. "There were quite a few of them. They ran off when I came." He motioned to the far side, the one that led to the big field. "Right there. They went through the hedge."

I stumbled across the sandy soil to the hedge, remembering the voices I'd heard there the day before. *"I'm sorry,"* I whispered to the bushes and the berries and the bugs and the bees. I stared at the hedge for a long time, like there was something I should do. When I finally walked back, Moose was in the same spot, still staring at his Little Field.

"There's a hole in the hedge," I said.

He nodded.

"I'm sorry, Moose."

Moose reached up and pulled his green cap low over his brow. "It's not your fault," he said in his kind, quiet way. "Not one bit of it."

But I knew it was.

"I shouldn't have run from the dog."

Moose squinted at the sky and let out a soft whistle. "No permanent damage. We just lost some berries, that's all. We'll just keep a better eye out next year, won't we? Might have to move the field again. We'll see."

The way he said that, the way he said *we* made me want to cry. After all that had happened, he still trusted me. He turned his back on his Little Field of berries. His most precious Little Field. "How about we get out of this sun?"

I followed Moose back across the meadow to the secret path. Halfway there, I stopped to pick something off the ground. My 3-D glasses. They were bent and crooked, probably trampled by running feet, but I put them in my pocket anyway.

Back at the sorting garage Bev was waiting, frozen where we left her. When Moose nodded, she came unfrozen. She shook her head angrily. "I'm calling the police."

My heart stopped. "What?"

"Theft," she explained.

I glanced quickly at Moose. The police! Would my brother be hauled away in a police car? Would he go to trial? Become a juvenile delinquent?

"Wait on calling the police," Moose said as he walked out of the garage and across the gravel drive. "I'll be out with the picking machine."

"Well I am calling the police!" she shouted after him. Then under her breath she muttered, "Oh, Moose."

As Moose drove off in a cloud of smoke and dust she grabbed my arm. "You come into the office and keep me company, Melissa. With all this craziness you missed your lunch. You can eat in front of the fan."

Lunch? Could there really be something as normal

as lunch? I said, "I'm not very hungry." *I should have told them,* I thought. *I should have told them I'd let it slip. I should have told them about my brother.*

I glanced down at my fingers, stained purple. I imagined a bright white plate in a small restaurant in France. Berries I'd picked, traveling all the way to France, and a table where two people would sit across from each other and speak about their lives, their childhoods, maybe make plans for the future. How unreal, I thought. To be so connected and so far apart. To our food, our families, and people all over the world. There was a dog that chased me and then licked my hand. How strange. How unreal.

"Bev," I said, "if you don't mind, I'll just wait over there." I pointed to our spot underneath the cherry tree. "I'll wait there until it's time to go home."

When I sat on my bucket I tried to concentrate on small things in front of me, like the ants climbing over the gravel. I watched a fat black beetle, stuck on its back, wiggle its legs in the air. When I took a twig and gently flipped it over, that's when I remembered the snakeskin. It had been with my buckets of berries!

I had wanted that snakeskin so badly. I'd wanted to take it home and keep it, to show Claude and Patrick its amazing perfect snake shape. I put my face in my hands and squeezed my eyes tightly so that tears wouldn't come. But that didn't work. They slid out anyway, two hot trails down my cheeks. I'd lost too much that day. There was no holding them back.

CHAPTER 38

THE SUN FOUND ITS WAY THROUGH THE LEAVES ON THE cherry tree. When it touched my head in the right spot I knew it was nearly quitting time. Footsteps crunched across the gravel and I looked up to see Bev. I was long cried out by then, but I wiped my eyes again anyway.

When Bev reached me she held out her hands. One was filled with crisp, new bills and the other with a frosty can. "Here's your pay," she said. "And I bet you're thirsty."

When I shook my head, the world started to spin. I was desperate for a glass of water, but I didn't feel like asking. I didn't deserve to ask either one of them for anything.

Bev shoved the bills into my hand and then hovered

over me, like she was waiting for something more. Finally she perched on the other overturned bucket. "I need to tell you something," she said.

"What is it? The police?"

"No. No police. But we'll be closing down after today. Moose just decided. He doesn't want any more kids out here this season. He'll bring extra machines in earlier than we'd planned. It was about time, with this heat. Machine picking makes the most sense anyway. I don't know what Moose was thinking, hiring kids again."

I cleared my throat. "Where is he?"

"He's still out in the field. He called to tell me the news."

"Will he be back before my mom picks me up?"

"I don't think so, hon."

I didn't know if I could speak without crying. Did this mean I would never see him again? I took a deep breath. "Could you just tell him something for me, then? Could you tell him—" but I didn't know how to finish the sentence. I tried to swallow the ache in my throat, but my mouth was too dry. Finally, I looked up at her helplessly.

She smiled and rested her hand on my shoulder. "He knows, hon. He knows. You were a wonderful worker and a true friend."

I shook my head. I couldn't get the right words out.

After Bev walked away I pulled the 3-D glasses from my pocket. At first, I thought they'd been destroyed, but after a little bending with my hands, I saw how they could probably be fixed with tape. And when the first of the pickers came shuffling up the hill, dragging extra clothes and clouds of dust, I propped the glasses on my face.

I watched the kids line up for their pay.

I watched them read the sign Bev had posted.

I felt a new anger in me rising up, ready to explode. I fixed my eyes on the tire-track road and waited for my brother. Finally, I saw him, coming up the hill with a group of kids, including Shauna in a red bikini top. I watched him laugh with them. I watched him motion with his arms. He didn't seem nervous or shy, and I couldn't even tell which leg had the limp. I tried to see him as if I didn't know him—didn't know how he looked when he cried or blew his nose or examined his face in the mirror, searching for pimples. If I weren't his sister to know all these things, I would think he was just like everyone else. How strange.

I saw one more thing that was strange. It was right before Mom pulled into the drive. I was on my feet, ready to march over to Patrick, ready to call him a thief and a liar. I took one wobbly step and was about to yell, "Hey!" when my eyes got all funny and full of sparkling lights.

I looked up to see what Bev had described to me: little dancing boys, chasing one another across the gravel drive.

I thought about Moose and Lyle as boys, with their game of rock, paper, scissors in the backseat of their daddy's car. I forgot about Patrick and turned instead toward them, those bright dancing lights. I put my arms out. I took a step and then another. And that's when my world went from spotty yellow to fuzzy gray.

Then, as the gravel drive came rushing to meet my face, the entire world turned black: thick, silent, absolute black.

CHAPTER 39

LATER THEY WOULD TELL ME I HAD A CASE OF HEAT exhaustion, which is one step away from heatstroke, and that I'd collapsed face-first on the gravel drive. They would tell me that any strange dancing light things or ghost boys were simply hallucinations that came from dehydration and too much sun on the top of my head.

As soon as we got home from the doctor, Mom whisked me to the couch. She placed an ice pack on my head, the part that wasn't covered by bandages. She brought me water, Popsicles, and lemonade.

"Too much sun can be a serious thing, Missy," she explained, again and again. "It's a good thing you didn't get heatstroke. Or sunstroke. People die from that, you know. Every year, they die."

"Oh, I know," I said, making sure Patrick could hear me. "Dog attacks, too."

"What?" Mom asked.

"Dog attacks. People die from so many things, like dog attacks. And betrayal. The heartbreak of betrayal. It's a dangerous world."

My mother came over and stared into my eyes. "Are you delirious again? Are you seeing things? Because if you are we're taking you straight back to the doctor."

I opened my eyes. "No, Mom. I'm just tired." And I was. I was tired all the way down to the center of my heart. "It was a hard day."

I looked straight at Patrick when I said it, and he spun around and stomped down the hallway. A moment later I heard the click of his bedroom door. I didn't see him the rest of the afternoon.

Mom let me eat my dinner on the couch, watching TV. And even though an old cowboy movie was on, she let me watch a game show. That's what falling face-first in gravel can do for you.

When Mom went to give Claude his bedtime bath, Patrick wandered into the living room. He stood next to the TV, his long skinny arms dangling stupidly at his sides.

Through clenched teeth I said, "You set a dog on me."

"It was a puppy. I knew it wouldn't hurt you."

"Then what did you expect to happen?"

"I thought you'd just take it back to the house, like a normal person does with a stray dog. We only used the puppy because we thought it would give us more time. We wanted more time to pick the field. We also wanted it to be a message to Moose. You know, since the puppy belonged to Lyle."

"How did you get in?"

"We cut a hole in the hedge, next to the big field. I figured out where you were after you said the monkey poo—"

I didn't let him finish. "How did you cut a hole? The hedge is enormous. And prickly."

"The Smith brothers brought a hedge clipper. We'd been cutting holes for days, looking for the Little Field. I'm really sorry about the dog, Missy. You know I am. I never wanted to scare you like that."

"The Little Field was mine. It was mine and you ruined it."

"It wasn't yours, Missy. It wasn't yours any more than it was mine. We were in a berry field, picking berries. That's all."

"But did you even see it? Did you even see how special it was?"

"We didn't hurt anything, Missy."

"Traitor!" I yelled.

"Do you even want to know my side of the story? There are always two sides."

"Monkey POO!" I yelled.

Mom called from the bathroom, "What is going on out there?"

"It's a game show, Mom," I shouted back. "One hundred thousand dollars."

Patrick shifted from one foot to the other. It made me happy to see him awkward and stupid and completely unlike the person he'd become in the blueberry field. "Like I said, we just picked some berries, Missy. It's not like a big terrible crime."

"You stole. You could have been arrested."

"But Moose stole those berries from Lyle, years ago. All we did was pick some buckets and put them on his porch. It was like a dare. It wasn't a big deal."

"How do you know? How do you know the truth about the field?"

"How do you?" he asked simply.

"Shut up!" I screamed. "Shut up, shut up, shut up!"

Mom called, "*What* is going on out there! Turn off that TV if it makes you scream like that."

Patrick turned and left the room, and I pulled the quilt up over my head.

I had wanted a showdown, just like in the movies. I had wanted to crush Patrick, to run him out of town or throw him in jail, to make him admit his betrayal and beg for forgiveness. I had wanted a good guy and a bad guy, a winner and a loser. I didn't get any of that.

When Mom tucked me in that night she ran her cool hand across my cheek. "How does your head feel?"

"All right," I said.

"Not too painful?"

"Not too bad," I said. "Mom, do you know where my glasses are? I was wearing them right before I passed out."

"I'm sorry, Missy. They probably got crushed when you fell. I'm sure someone threw them away. It was a crazy moment."

"I know, Mom," I said, trying not to cry about my glasses, and the snakeskin, too. "It's a crazy world."

"Not so crazy," she said as she bent over and kissed me good night. "Just some crazy moments here and there."

But alone in the dark, my head started to spin again. It *was* a crazy world. It was crazy that I could trust a complete stranger more than I could trust my own brother; that I could trust a complete stranger more than my own *father*. Just what *could* a person count on around here? I was about to roll off the bed to get my feet on solid ground when one answer came to me: food.

We all needed food. We counted on food. I took a deep breath and forced myself to think of all the things I had learned about food—how simple it could be, and how complex. How quiet it could be, growing in a field, but at the same time how loud it all was—the earth so alive with movement and sound and color and smell. I forced myself to conjure the sky as it was over a field full of green, the biggest, widest stretch of pure color I'd ever seen.

The more I thought about the things I knew, all the good things there could be, and about my place in those good things, the spinning finally stopped and my head was left with the sweet sound of Claude sleeping in the bed across from mine. And with that simple and perfect sound, I was finally able to fall asleep.

CHAPTER 40

CONSTANCE'S MOTHER, WHO ALWAYS GIVES GOOD advice, said I shouldn't worry too much about it. She said that everything happens for a reason and that I would someday know the reason and that the dog would probably be all right, too. But when she said, "And honey, you're only twelve. There are some things you can't yet understand." I swallowed hard so I wouldn't start to cry all over again.

It was the first time Constance's mother had ever said the wrong thing, and her words were about as far away from me as any words had ever been. Which meant that even Constance's mother, who told people's fortunes for a living, had no idea. So I said, "I'd better go. I have some things to do. Maid of honor things."

Constance's mother nodded. "People get crazy when it comes to weddings." She bent close and stared at my bandaged face. "Did you end up having stitches?"

I shook my head. "The nurse just had to pick out gravel with these tiny tweezers. It took a long time."

She put her arm around my shoulders and gave me a squeeze. "Well, the girls will be home next week, in time for the wedding. I'm sure you'll have the bandages off by then, too."

"Maybe," I said. I knew that it wouldn't matter. That I didn't care. That with my plan in effect, no one would be looking at my face anyway.

I had snuck out while Mom was at the store with Claude, snuck my bike out of the garage and rode it over. I knew, of course, that Constance wasn't there, but I needed to talk to someone, someone outside my own family.

Even though I'd left a note, Mom was still a worried mess by the time I came home. "Missy! You shouldn't have been out! Don't you remember what the doctor said? How are you feeling? How is your head? Drink this orange juice."

"Where's Patrick?"

"Sit down here."

I sat at the table and took a sip of juice. "Where's Patrick?"

"He's at your dad's, helping with things. Something about the backyard and a gazebo for the wedding."

"Oh." Gazebo.

"You look better today." Mom's worried wrinkle smoothed out. "Just like the doctor said you would."

"Great," I said.

"How do your scrapes feel?"

I patted the bulky bandages. "Like I fell face-first in a gravel driveway."

Mom set out a cup for Claude and a plate piled with honey toast for us both. "Yum, yum," I said to my brother in a Donald Duck voice, and he laughed. "So did Dad want me to help, too?"

"No, Missy. He said you should rest. Like the doctor said. You need a few days' rest."

"The big day is coming up," I said. "Maybe I won't be better by then. Maybe I'll have to stay here."

"You'll be better," Mom said. "Although we do need to buy you a dress."

"I have a dress."

Mom's right eyebrow shot up.

"Tessa bought me a dress."

Mom looked at me funny but didn't say another word about it.

I picked up a piece of honey toast, noticing how my

fingers were stained blue at the tips. I swallowed hard and said, "I need to go back to the field."

"Maybe next summer. They're done with pickers this season."

"I want to go back today. I need to say good-bye. I didn't get a chance—" My voice broke, thinking about it all—the Little Field, my 3-D glasses, that perfect snakeskin, the puppy. But especially Moose, bent over his daddy's precious plants.

"You need to stay out of the sun."

"Mom. Please. They were my friends," I said. "They *are* my friends."

"No, Missy—"

I wiped my eyes with the back of my hand. "Well, I have to get my money." It was a lie, Bev had already paid me, but I was desperate. "I didn't get my money. And I'm afraid if I don't go today, they'll forget. Please, Mom. Just drive me out there. I'll just get my money and go. Please. I earned it. I worked hard. It's only fair."

"Maybe tomorrow, Missy," she said. "Or the next day. Today you rest."

CHAPTER 41

ALL THAT DAY I RESTED ON THE COUCH, WATCHING one black-and-white cowboy movie after another. On the second day, when Patrick went to the lake, I decided I would stay on the couch the rest of the summer. Maybe the rest of my life.

I sipped ice water and orange juice and studied the showdowns in each movie, imagining Patrick as the bad guy that I chase out of town. But then my imaginings turned to real-life color as I pictured Patrick at the lake, among the bikinis and cool swim trunks, doing cannonballs and being king of chicken fights. I worked myself into a fury, thinking about it all. *Swimming at the lake! In his new swimsuit he got from the mall! With money from Moose and Bev! Praying Mantis Boy!*

By the time he came home, smelling like sunscreen and potato chips, I hated him even more.

On the afternoon of my third couch day, Mom called the doctor who said to come right in. After looking in my mouth and eyes and poking me and asking me some questions, he told her I was perfectly fine, that my heat exhaustion was not an issue, and that he could find absolutely nothing wrong with me. He peeled off the bandages and said that everything was healing nicely but to keep it covered for a few more days.

"But she just lies on the couch," Mom said. "Like she has no energy. Could it be a concussion?"

He shook his head. "There's no sign of a concussion. Is she under any stress right now?" He asked it as if I wasn't even in the room. And while I stared at the shiny stethoscope hanging around his neck, I saw my mother nod meekly in its reflection.

"I'm maid of honor at my father's upcoming wedding," I said loudly. "I'm stressed that my hair won't look right."

That got me sent me to the waiting room so they could talk privately.

The ride home was silent until Mom asked if I'd like to talk about anything. I told her, "The blueberry field,

Mom. I'd like to talk about that. You said I could go back out, but then you always come up with an excuse."

"Fair enough, Missy," she said. "You are right. To-morrow. First thing tomorrow."

The next morning, on the way out to the field, Mom made me put on a hat and wear it even in the car. Patrick was gone by the time I got up, to the lake already, on his bike. She asked, "How are you feeling?"

"Fine, Mom. Like the doctor said, I'm fine." But when we pulled into the drive and I heard the familiar crunch of gravel under tires, and I saw myself falling face-first all over again, I felt about as un-fine as a person could feel. I said, "Can you just drop me off and come back later? I don't know how long I'll be."

Mom wrinkled her forehead. "I'll drive around for a few minutes. So Claude doesn't get bored. But only for a few minutes, Missy. It shouldn't take you long to get your money."

"More boo-berries?" Claude asked.

"Not today, Claude," I said, waving him off. "There's no picking today."

The air was thick around me. Even on that short walk across the gravel drive I could feel it weighing me down. The lights in the garage were off, but as I turned toward the office, I heard a familiar and welcoming voice. "Well, here's a sight for old eyes."

I smiled and walked up to the office window where Al sat, on Bev's stool, drinking coffee from his red plastic cup. "Hi, Al. I didn't expect to see you up here."

"Now that you kids are gone they don't need me down in the field. So I'm stuck in this tiny room, answering phones and making sure there's not a fire. And I sort berries, when they come in. We're all sorting berries, day and night. What are you hiding under those bandages? Did you get a tattoo?"

I laughed. "Just some gravel marks."

"How are you feeling? We were all worried about you."

"I'm fine," I said.

"Do we owe you some money?"

"No, Bev paid me already. But I didn't get to say good-bye." Which was only half of what I needed to say.

"Moose and Bev are out with the picking machines. Don't expect them back anytime soon. I'll tell them you were here, though. To say good-bye. I know they both hope to see you next picking season."

I leaned against the side of the house, feeling my head start to spin.

"Are you okay, Melissa? Do you need to sit down?"

"I'm okay. I just came out to ask something. I need to know something."

"I'll tell you if I can."

"Well," I said. "How can this be?"

"What be?"

"You know. Everything." I motioned toward the hedge. "What's the truth about Moose and Lyle?"

Al shook his head as he gazed across the gravel drive. Finally he said, "Moose always loved the fields, but Lyle never seemed to want to stick around. I remember working here as a kid—I was older than they were, but friendly enough with both of them. Lyle took off as soon as he could, but then came back right before their father died. That meant the world to the old man, but it made things harder for Moose. Especially when Lyle suddenly had his own ideas about running the place."

"Moose told me some of it," I said. "Out in the field. He told me they had different ideas about how to farm it."

"It's just about the oldest story in the book. Hey, enough. Why don't we talk about something else?"

How could I tell him what this meant to me? That it wasn't just someone else's story anymore?

Al filled his red plastic cup with more coffee. He looked done talking, and I knew my mom would be back soon. "Al," I said, "I came out here to tell Moose something. It's important. I didn't tell him that day, the day it all happened. So I need you to tell him. I need him to know. It's my fault. It's all my fault."

"I don't see how it could be your fault, Melissa. No one blames you."

"But see, I let it slip. Moose asked me to be careful and I let it slip. My brother figured it out because, well, I wanted to show off. And I knew they were looking for it . . ." My voice trailed away and I closed my eyes.

"I should have told Moose that morning, that I'd given it away. I could have stopped it. See, it really is my fault. I gave away the secret."

Al didn't answer for a long time. When I opened my eyes, he was looking across the gravel drive to the hedge, like maybe he didn't want to see me or speak to me ever again. "How's the dog, Al?"

"The puppy?" He chuckled. "Oh, he's fine. Lyle just makes a big deal out of everything. He's always been that way."

I was relieved. "That's good. Well, my mom will be back soon. Tell Moose what I told you. Tell him I'll pay for the damage done, even if it takes my whole life. Tell him I hate my brother and will never forgive him for sneaking into the Little Field and stealing all those berries."

Al chuckled. "Don't hate your brother, Melissa. He's a good kid."

"Tell me the truth, Al. It's Lyle's fault, isn't it? Moose wasn't lying, was he? Because that's what my brother said. He said Moose stole from Lyle."

"Oh, it's all so long ago. I'm an old man now. What do I remember? Anyway, Moose knew he was taking a chance, putting a kid out in that field. Maybe he wanted Lyle to find it."

"What?"

"There are a lot of things that can hold us together, that's all."

"I don't understand—"

"I'm not saying it's right, but maybe it's their way of staying boys. Boys playing Capture the Flag. Boys wrestling in the backyard. Boys racing across the field. Only when they were boys it wasn't a mean thing. Most kids don't play mean. They were friends when they were boys. They grew up and didn't know how to do it like kids do, take what works and leave the rest. But don't feel too sorry for them, Melissa. People make their choices. They've chosen not to be brothers in the real sense. There's nothing anyone can do about it now. They wouldn't even know where to start."

I felt such a piercing sadness at that moment, thinking of Moose and his brother. "I loved being out there, Al," I said quietly. "It wasn't about the money."

"It's never been about the money for Moose, either."

"Did Moose steal the little bushes from Lyle? Is that what started it?"

"I guess it all depends on which side of the hedge you're standing on."

"But you're standing on this side."

"I happen to be on this side. But if you look closely, you'll see I'm just about as in the middle as a person can be."

"What about Lyle?"

"Lyle just felt left out. That's how I see it. He never really liked to farm, and he felt left out. And so he went away. Took off just as soon as he could."

There had to be more to it than that. There had to be!

The spinning in my head was back. I grabbed on to the edge of the window and held on tight. I heard myself saying, "I loved those tiny bushes. I loved the sandy soil and the flat, open field. I loved hearing the grasshoppers in the grass and the bees humming around the blossoms. I felt . . . complete. Like a bee must feel when it's doing what it was born to do without anything getting in its way. Complete. And I don't feel that way very much in my life anymore. My life is in little pieces."

I'd just said more about how I felt than I'd said since my father moved out. I said words that I hadn't been able to, not even to my brother or Constance and Allie. I pinched my arm hard and concentrated on the sharp feeling of pain so I wouldn't cry about the bigger one.

Al looked down at his big, dry hands. He started to whistle a tune. Had he even heard me?

"Please, Al. Just tell me."

Al must have recognized something near desperation in my voice. "I've never told anyone this before," he said. "Never thought it was anyone's business. But I'll tell you, Melissa. After I do, you might think you know who's right and who's wrong. But you won't. It's more complicated than that. Will you remember that? Will you promise to remember that?"

"Yes," I said. "I promise."

"Okay," he said. And then he told me. Most of it I'd known already, how Lyle had made it back to the farm before his father died. How the boys had tried farming together, but each had such definite ideas that it had been nearly impossible. So they'd agreed to divide the farm in half. Lyle left again to clear up his business and by the time he got back, the hedges were planted.

But then he got to the new part, the part no one knew. And he told me. And when he was done, I wished he hadn't.

Al said, "You know when there's a piece of cake that two people need to share? One cuts it down the middle and the other one gets to choose the piece. That keeps everything fair, right?"

"Yes," I said.

"Well, Moose divided up the farm and then let Lyle pick his side. Only Moose deliberately made one side a bit better than the other. And Lyle picked the better side. Still fair?"

"I guess."

"Except there was something Lyle didn't know. He didn't know about their father's Little Field. He never knew it existed. Moose cut it up so that the Little Field was on the slightly smaller side. He gambled that Lyle would pick the better side, leaving him with the Little Field. And his gamble paid off. Lyle looked at the map of the fields and picked what appeared to be the better choice. He got what he wanted. Eventually though, over the years, Lyle caught on that Moose had something special. Word got out this way or that. Those berries suddenly got to be a hot item—they weren't at first, you know—not when Moose divided up the farm. He just loved that field because it was straight from his father's hands. And, well, you pretty much know the rest, don't you?"

It wasn't a big story, like you'd see in the movies. It

wasn't surprising, either. It was just, as a grown-up might say, "one of those things." But I couldn't help think in terms of right and wrong, even though I'd promised Al I wouldn't.

"So it was Moose's fault," I said as soon as he'd finished. As soon as I could trust my voice to speak. "He *did* steal it from Lyle."

"Well, there are two ways to think of it. While Lyle spent his young adulthood out seeing the world, Moose was right here, sweating on this farm. He helped his father develop those bushes. And the entire farm was originally supposed to be his, remember? All his. For the longest time, Lyle hadn't wanted anything to do with it. So, that's another way of looking at it."

"But, still. It wasn't fair what he did. It was a trick. And a lie."

Al said firmly, "You promised not to make any judgments."

"I can't help it."

"It was a long time ago and a lot has happened since. Moose wasn't after more money. Like I said, it wasn't even valuable when he divided everything up."

"It doesn't matter," I said.

Al shook his head sadly. "Everyone needs to find a way to make peace with the humanity of others. If you can't do that, well, you've seen exactly what can happen. Maybe that will be your bigger lesson out here, Missy."

Who was Al to tell me about lessons? What did he know about my life?

"I have to go," I said. I turned around sharply. When I heard him calling my name, I didn't look back.

It was only when I was in the car and we were driving along Old Farm Road with the cool breeze on my face did I realize Al had called me by my real name. For the first time ever, he'd called me Missy.

CHAPTER 42

WHEN WE GOT HOME I DOVE STRAIGHT FOR THE COUCH and pulled the quilt up over my head. "Too much sun again," I told my mom, so she tiptoed around, bringing me snacks and mint iced tea. I slept there that night and the next day and the next night, too.

Even Claude knew something was wrong. He came with little gifts—a stick from the backyard, a tiny knight's helmet from the castle set—and wanted to snuggle under the covers, but after less than a minute he'd wiggle out shouting, "Too hot! Too hot!"

Then my friends returned from camp. They called the minute they came home and every day after that but I always told Mom to tell them I didn't feel so well, that

I was sleeping, that I'd call back. Finally, they just rode their bikes over. Luckily I heard them first, laughing up the drive, and I made a dash for my bedroom, just as the doorbell rang.

Heart pounding, I closed the door and then quickly dove underneath my bed. Expertly, I arranged myself in Intruder mode and lay perfectly still, trying to calm my loud breath and pounding heart.

"Missy? Missy?" I heard Mom's voice, calling through the house. "Missy?" She opened my bedroom door.

Through the tiny hole in Claude's old baby blanket I could see six feet enter the room. "Missy?" Mom said again. And then, "Well, I have no idea where she went, girls."

"Just tell her we're going to the lake today. We're going tomorrow, too. We want her to come."

"I'll do that. I know she'd love it."

Wrong. I wouldn't love it. I imagined them both in the bright swimsuits they bought new for camp, leaping off the diving board, laughing with new friends, just like they described in their letters.

"She's been having a hard time lately," Mom said quietly.

"We know." That was Constance's voice. "My mom explained things."

Oh, great. Now everyone was talking about me.

"I know she'll want you both to be at the wedding."

Wrong again!

"My mom told us about that, too," said Constance. "We were so surprised."

Allie added, "Missy didn't even write to us about it. And now she's not calling us back or anything."

"You know, this wedding isn't easy for her. Maybe that's why she's not calling."

"But we always call one another back!"

"I know," Mom said. "But a lot has happened. She even lost her glasses. She was wearing them when she fell. I'm sure someone just threw them away."

"What?"

"Those funny glasses you girls always wear. The ones you got at the movies."

"Oh, those. We don't wear them anymore." Allie's voice. Allison. With a little laugh, of course.

Get out! I wanted to shout. *Get out! This is my room and I want you all out!*

As though they heard me, six feet turned and left my room. I watched the spot where they had been, more empty than ever. I heard the door shut and moments later, chatter down the driveway as Constance and Allie rode away on their bikes.

How easy it should be, to crawl out from under my

bed and run to catch up with them. It used to be so easy, anyway. So why wasn't it anymore? What had happened? What was happening? Why was I so frozen? Was I under some sort of weird spell?

I stayed like that, frozen in my Intruder spot, until Claude's little feet wandered into the room. I watched them come straight for the bed. A moment later, his big head appeared underneath. *"Missy?"* he whispered, his eyes wide. He sucked on his fingers and stared at the spot where my one eye peeked out of his old baby blanket.

I yanked the blanket off my face. I couldn't hide from Claude. "Yes?"

"Come out."

I thought for a moment. "Did Mom tell you I was here?"

He nodded.

"Okay," I said. And I rolled out.

CHAPTER 43

"GET YOUR BATHING SUIT," MOM SAID. "I'M DROPPING you off at the lake today."

"What? No!"

Patrick looked up from his breakfast cereal. "Will you drop me off, too?"

"Of course," Mom said. "Although I'm impressed with how you've been riding your bike every day. That's a long ride!"

Patrick flexed his calf muscles. "Look," he said. "From all the hills."

I bent forward and squinted at his legs. "I don't see anything," I said. "Not one thing. And anyway, I'm not going. I don't feel well. I believe I *do* have a concussion."

"You don't have a concussion. You never did. You don't feel well because you've been sitting on that couch, underneath a quilt, watching too much TV. The doctor said you are fine, and you are now going to get out and enjoy the summer. Your friends will both be there, so finish your breakfast and grab your suit and towel." I knew the look on Mom's face meant there was no way out.

The last time my friends and I were there, the summer before, I had introduced them to the little store and we pooled our money to buy a party-size bag of potato chips and a gigantic root beer. I took them to the fishing dock, the one where my dad taught me to cast a line. I remember we put on our 3-D glasses and dangled our arms over the side of the dock and stared deep into the lake. Then we pushed our Spectacular Buttons and studied the teenagers across the water.

Thinking about all that, on the drive out to the lake, I started to feel a twinge of excitement about seeing my friends. It was the lake, after all. Next to the blueberry field, it was the greatest place on earth.

They were sitting on the very end of the swimming dock, and when they saw me they jumped up and sprinted all the way to shore. "Missy!" they cried together, their bare feet slapping against slippery wood. *Pat-pat-pat-pat-pat.*

And then, *hug-hug-hug-hug-hug.*

I hugged them back, just as hard as they were hugging me, and then we jumped and jumped and jumped. Every other thing—every terrible and wonderful and impossible and mysterious thing—disappeared the moment my two best friends threw their arms around me and shrieked my actual true name. *Missy, Missy, Missy, Missy, Missy.*

"Missy! Where have you been?" Allie was the first to pull back from the hug and scrutinize. "We have been calling you every day!"

Constance kept her arm around my shoulders and said, "She's here now, A. It doesn't matter."

"A?" I said.

"That's what they called me at camp. I think I'm going to keep it." And then the two of them burst out laughing at the exact same time.

"Oh my gosh," Constance said. "The other Allison was so mad!"

"What?" I said.

"I know. Remember how she was all, *whatever!* with the apple?"

"And then her face whenever you got called first because of alphabetization?" They cracked up again. "Oh, Missy, you should have seen it!"

I nodded and made my mouth smile, but what I

wanted was to go back to that first moment, the running-down-the-dock moment and the tight huddle when there was no one else in the world but the three-of-us-forever moment.

They led me back down the slippery dock, to the end, where I noticed, for the first time, three other girls. "Everyone," Constance announced proudly, "this is Missy!"

"Hi, Missy," the other three girls said. Then they smiled at me, waiting.

While Allie pointed out introductions—"Mia, Natalie, Jasmine"—I said hi three times. Hi, Hi, Hi. After that, though, no one knew what to do.

"We were all in the same cabin together," Constance explained.

"Oh, that's so great," I said.

Constance and Allie plopped back down, making a tight little circle with one space left for me. I was still holding my bag with my towel and sunscreen and some berry-picking money. As I stood there, I felt my swimsuit shrink up or my body expand, or both at the same time. I tried to remember how long I'd had it—at least two years? I was suddenly a fleshy giant, wearing one piece of faded blue fabric that rode up high in the back and low in the front. I was sticking out everywhere! How did I not notice it before?

I sat down in their circle and pulled my legs in tight, trying to hide my chest that, for the first time ever, made me feel embarrassed. There was just too much body going on! When did that happen?

The other girls, including my friends, were all wearing two-piece suits, brightly colored and cheerful looking. "What?" I said, when I realized that all eyes were on me, waiting for some kind of response to a question I hadn't heard.

Mia or Natalie or Jasmine repeated the question, "Are you going to come to camp with us next year? You should!"

"Maybe," I said, shrugging. Which was the wrong thing to do because when I moved, even a tiny bit, my suit pulled tighter, revealing even more of me. I hunched over and said again, "Maybe."

Constance said, "Missy, tell us all about your summer. My mom told us some things." She turned to the group. "Missy's dad is getting married."

Allie added, "Missy is maid of honor."

The three other girls made quick chipmunk-like noises, causing my already jumbled brain to get even more confused.

"What are you going to wear?" Mia or Natalie or Jasmine asked.

"Um, I have a dress," I said.

"What's it like?"

"Um, it has skulls," I said.

There was a moment of silence and then everyone laughed. "She *is* funny," one of the girls said. "Just like you guys said."

"No, but really. What does it look like?"

I glanced across the water, to the dock in the middle where all the teenagers were goofing around. "You guys want to go swimming?" I could just make out Patrick, pushing another guy into the water. Then a girl pushed in Patrick. I couldn't tell if it was Shauna.

"Out to the teenager dock?"

"No," I said quickly. "Not there. We could go to the logs and try to balance."

And just like that we were all in the water, swimming and splashing our way to the logs and things didn't feel so bad anymore.

The line of logs were chained together and made a boundary between the lifeguarded swimming area and the rest of the lake. They were fun because they spun around and were slippery, so we had log-balancing contests like the lumberjacks did in olden times.

We scrambled to climb on the logs and straightened to standing, balanced and slipped, splashed into the water and then, laughing our heads off, scrambled up to do it all again. I didn't even mind my swimsuit so much when we were playing like that.

The other girls were nice and laughed about everything. They went to the other middle school in town but told me we would all hang out. They had made a pact with Constance and Allie. CFF. Cabin Friends Forever. "You, too, of course," they said to me.

"Great," I said. I told them I'd be right back, that I had to use the bathroom. Then I dove down deep and swam for the dock.

CHAPTER 44

OUT BEHIND THE LITTLE STORE, I FOUND A SECRET hiding place. Wrapped in a towel, sitting on a smooth stump of a tree, I closed my eyes and listened to the sounds all around me: the echoing shouts of kids swimming; the wind rustling the leaves; the screen door banging whenever anyone walked into the store; voices through the open window asking for worms and sunscreen and sandwiches. I had meant to swim back out to them, I really had, but once I was on land, wrapped in my towel, I felt better. Safer. And that's where I wanted to stay.

So that's where Constance and Allie found me, sitting on the stump, listening to birds. "Missy! What? We've been looking for you everywhere!"

"Why didn't you come back, Missy?"

At first, I couldn't speak. I looked at their bare feet covered in dirt and grass and pine needles and even campfire soot, making me know that they really had looked everywhere for me. Their toenails, peeking through all that grime, were painted the same sparkly pink. "I don't think we're friends anymore," I said finally.

"Of course we're friends," Allie said.

"Best friends," said Constance.

"You two are best friends. And now you have other best friends." I took in a deep shaky breath. "You don't even know what I've been doing this summer."

"Because you haven't told us!" said Allie. "We know some things, from your mom and Constance's mom. We know you fainted."

"We know you baked a pie," Constance said. "I kept the letter. I'm going to try to bake one, too."

My pie. My pie seemed like from a different summer.

"You probably made new friends, too," Allie said. "But that doesn't change things between us."

"Everything is changed between us." I stared at twenty pink toes. "Everything is different. Remember when you were leaving for camp? Remember the thing about our 3-D glasses?"

The toes did not move.

"Well, did you even bring them to camp? Did you wear them? Because I did. I wore them and I saw things. Amazing things."

I stopped. I sounded stupid and I knew it.

"Missy." Constance plopped down in front of me, right in the dirt. Allie plopped right next to her. Their cute suits would get dirty. "No, we didn't bring our glasses, but that doesn't mean we're not friends."

My throat was so tight I couldn't speak. What made people friends, anyway? Had Moose and I been friends? Bev?

Constance said, "Remember when we built the time travel machine and we were sure it would work?"

I smiled.

"And remember when we ran away?" Allie said. "And we tried to be the Boxcar Children?"

I laughed.

"Do we still do those things?"

"No," I said.

"So that's the point. We change what we do but we're still friends. Right? Okay?"

I nodded. "Right. Okay."

They tried to drag me back to the lake, but I lied and said my mom was on her way. "Next time," I said. "Next time I'll stay longer. I still have a concussion."

So they left me there but first, through the open store window, I heard them in the store, deciding on a party-size bag of potato chips and a gigantic root beer. I heard Allie say, "What is even up with her?"

And Constance said something back, but I couldn't make out what it was.

What was up with me was this: When they'd asked about the things we used to do, the games we used to play, my real answer, the one inside my head, had been different from the smiling one I'd given them.

What's so wrong about building a time machine?

What's so wrong about playing Boxcar Children?

What's so wrong about wearing 3-D glasses with the lenses popped out?

What's so wrong about keeping things the same forever?

Those were my real answers. The answers I couldn't say out loud to my so-called best friends.

CHAPTER 45

"I THINK I'LL WEAR THIS COUCH TO THE WEDDING," I announced to my mother, the day before the big day. "Or at least this quilt. It's very pretty."

"Get up and take a shower," she said.

"I can't." I pointed to the TV. "The bad guys just rode into town."

Mom was folding laundry. She stacked huge piles of towels and socks and shirts on the back of the couch. When she ran out of space, she piled washcloths and sheets on top of my legs. "Constance and Allie called again," she said. "They want to see you. They suggested a movie this time."

"Because the lake was so fun?"

My mom sighed. "Okay, Missy. Do you want to talk about things? Do you want to talk about tomorrow?"

"No," I said.

"You will get up. You will wash your hair. You will be on time. This is important."

"I know," I said. "It's very important. That's why I'm resting up today."

Mom looked worried. Really worried. And Dad was off somewhere, worried about other things, like gazebos and cake and parking spots for guests. Those things. I felt bad about being the cause of that unattractive crease between my mother's eyebrows, but there was no way I was getting off the couch until I absolutely had to.

If it weren't for the dress, my maid of honor war dress, I don't think I would have been able to get up at all. I couldn't wait to see the looks on their faces—Dad and Tessa and all the happy guests—when I marched down the aisle wearing it. Just thinking about it in the dark corner of my closet, still with the tag that said Looks Can Kill, gave me the giggles. Not the happy giggles, but at least I wasn't crying.

That night, the night before the wedding, I slept on the couch and woke up sweaty after dreams I couldn't remember. When the light coming from the window let me know it was finally morning, I opened my eyes and thought *this is the day.* I could hear water running in the bathroom—someone in the shower already. This was the day.

I slipped out from underneath the quilt and stretched my arms over my head. I had a plan, suddenly, to make coffee for Mom and scrambled eggs for us all, and I was surprised at how good it felt to be up, doing something. When Mom came into the kitchen she was surprised, too. "Missy," she said, "you're up!"

"I'm up, Mom," I said. "How about some coffee."

She nodded her head with quick, grateful movements. I could see her eyes filling with tears and the worried crease between her eyebrows beginning to soften.

Patrick came in, toweling off his wet hair and smelling of something new but familiar. "What's that smell?" I asked.

"What smell? Shampoo?"

"No, it's something else. But I can't place it." I went over and stood close. "It's shaving cream!" I shouted. "Shaving cream!"

Patrick's ears turned red. "So?"

"So what—you're shaving now?"

"Leave him alone, Missy," Mom said with a smile. "Come and eat these eggs you made. They look delicious."

Claude came running down the hallway, shrieking with the joy of being completely naked. With skin still warm and pink from his bath, he looked like a sweet little pig. This is my family, I said to myself. The rest doesn't matter.

"Go jump in the shower," Mom said. "We can't be late."

"When are we being picked up?"

"I'm driving you."

"What?" I was surprised.

"I'm driving you."

I couldn't imagine her driving up to the house on the day of the wedding, dropping us off and then driving away. Somehow that just seemed too much. Even Dad wouldn't ask that of her. He'd already asked some cousin of his to pick us up and babysit Claude while we got ready to do our best man/maid of honor chores. It had been planned like that for weeks.

"What about that cousin?" I said. "Dad's weird cousin from—"

"Eat your eggs."

"You told me to jump in the shower."

"Then do something, Missy!" Mom shouted angrily. "Just do *something*!"

We all froze. Mom never shouted like that. She would get angry sometimes but she never shouted at us. I looked down at my plate of eggs. The thought of eating them made my stomach lurch.

"I'll be quick," I said tightly. "Don't want to be late for my father's wedding." And with that I went straight to the bathroom and stood under the steaming hot water until a fist pounding on the door told me it was time to stop.

CHAPTER 46

THE RIDE TO THE WEDDING COULD HAVE BEEN A RIDE to anywhere. We were clean and showered but dressed in normal clothes, since our fancy wedding outfits were already hanging in closets at Dad's house. Patrick had a bag packed with extra clothes for Claude, since he couldn't stay clean for more than ten minutes at a time. And in my backpack, of course, was the secret weapon dress from the dark corner of my closet.

"So why are you driving us, Mom?" I asked after we'd been riding in silence for several minutes. "I'm just wondering."

"I told you. Things got a little mixed up. Your dad's cousin couldn't come as early as she thought so your dad called last night and asked if I would do this. It's no big deal." I could hear her voice trying extra hard to be casual. "I do have a favor, though."

Patrick asked, "What is it, Mom?"

"Can you two just get Claude into the house fairly quickly. You know."

I knew. "You don't want to see Dad, do you? On his second wedding day."

Mom said, "It's not that. It's not that at all." But I knew it was.

Of course, the moment we pulled up I realized the folly of that plan. Dad was already out front, talking to some parking guy or catering guy—one of the many guys hired to make the day go smoothly. He was dressed in his tux pants and a white shirt, but not the jacket or tie. I saw his face get tight, just for a moment, before he gave Mom a friendly wave on his way to the car.

Mom sighed and glanced at herself in the rearview mirror. Then she turned to us and forced a bright smile. "You all look great," she said as she opened the door to greet my father.

My mom had spent so much time getting us all bathed and shiny that she hadn't had time to put on her new face goop from the mall, or even the free lipstick. When she got out of the car I looked at her, really looked. Her hair was pulled back in a ponytail and she'd thrown on a plain white T-shirt and faded jeans. Her cheeks were flushed, her cheekbones high and delicate. She was beautiful, like the heroine of a tragic and heartbreaking tale. If she only had a horse or a cape, I thought, she could be on the cover of one of Bev's paperback novels.

My throat was so tight I could barely breathe. I got out, grabbed my backpack and threw my arms around her. *"I'm glad you're my mom,"* I whispered in her ear. For some reason it felt like I was saying a big good-bye, like we were all going on a long trip and leaving her behind.

She held me tight. "I'm proud of you, Missy," she said back. "Have *fun* today."

I thought of the dress wadded up in my backpack and nodded. I would certainly have fun. And she'd hear all about it later. There would even be photographs.

While Patrick hugged our mom, I stepped over to the sidewalk. After his good-bye, Patrick came and stood next to me. Together we waited for Dad to get Claude.

I watched my parents carefully. Would there be a moment when Dad suddenly remembered his other wedding day? Would he think, *This is the person I cut that cake with, all those years ago*? Or do you turn those things off—close them like a book you once loved but couldn't possibly read again? And if so, are our lives made up of books like that? Entire collections of moments that makes us who we are, but are impossible to keep open all at once?

Mom leaned into the backseat and unbuckled Claude. Even though he was getting too big for it, she lifted him out and held him tight. When Claude saw Dad he reached his arms out happily.

"Come here, Mr. Claudio," Dad said softly, giving him a squeeze. "Thanks, Claudia." And I crossed my fingers hoping he wouldn't say something terrible like, "I'm sorry," and he didn't, not even in his voice.

But they did stay there, just for a moment. They stayed like that, both holding on to Mr. Claude. And they smiled, over his big round head. "He's getting so big," Dad said. "You're getting so big, Claude."

And Mom said, "He's very excited about the wedding cake."

"The wedding cake? You're excited about the wedding cake, Mr. Claudio?"

Claude's face turned red as he squirmed his way out of their arms. "Put me DOWN!" he roared.

They both laughed. "He reminds me of Missy at that age," Mom said.

Dad nodded. "Except Missy was louder." They laughed again, remembering.

It was almost too much to look at, and yet, it was what I had been waiting to see. After all the months of hearing them say it to us, *We're still your parents together,* I finally saw it with my own eyes. It was in the look they shared over the top of Claude's head. It was in how they remembered me.

We were a family. Not the family I wanted us to be, but still a family. My mom and dad might not be together in most ways, but they both loved Mr. Claudio. They loved him together. And they loved me, too. And Patrick.

It wasn't the moment I'd been secretly dreaming about, the one where Dad, suddenly coming to his senses, whisks Mom off her feet and carries her to the backyard. And while Tessa runs away screaming and crying and ripping the hair out of her very own head, the minister calmly performs their marriage ceremony all over again.

This actual moment was small—here and gone before anyone could have snapped a photograph. But it was real. And it was ours.

I knew that my mom would get in the car and drive away and that my dad would go to the backyard and marry someone named Tessa. But the fact that it had been there at all seemed to unravel the terrible knot that had become my stomach. Right at that moment, I couldn't hate my dad. Not even on his wedding day.

I turned and started up the sidewalk. I had to leave before my mom drove off in the car all alone, headed back to an empty house. I had to leave while there was still a tiny bit of magic in the air.

CHAPTER 47

"YOU'RE JOKING, RIGHT? THIS IS A JOKE?" PATRICK stood in front of the bathroom's full-length mirror, adjusting his silver-green tie while I wrestled with my Looks Can Kill, skull and bone, spandex, camouflage minidress.

Every time I pulled the dress down to my knees, it managed to creep up to my thighs in about three seconds. After the fourth try, Patrick started to laugh.

"Thanks," I said. "Thanks a lot." I dashed back across the hall to my room.

Patrick followed. "Missy, I wasn't laughing at you. You look, well—isn't that what you want? Don't you want to make a statement?"

I fell down on the bed and covered my face with my hands. "I don't know anymore. I don't know. I just didn't want to wear a dress that Tessa picked out for me. And I wanted to hurt them somehow. But I don't know."

"You don't have to, Missy. You don't have to do anything they want you to do."

"What?" I sat up straight. Patrick looked good. Respectable. Sharp in his dark suit and pressed white shirt.

He said, "Do you think this is easy for *me*?"

"Of course it's easy. You act like it is. You're the one who blames me for making things hard. You even said it. You said I make it hard for you."

"Maybe I'm just not as brave as you are, Missy." He looked away quickly so that I couldn't see his face, and I suddenly wondered if he, too, wanted to be anywhere but here, stuck in this room and wearing a fancy wedding suit. I stood up and the dress immediately crept up my thighs. I yanked it back down.

"Wait!" Patrick said. He left the room suddenly, like he'd just remembered something important. A moment later he was back, carrying a long plastic bag. "Mom told me to give this to you. If you weren't feeling sure of yourself."

"What?"

"I don't know. That's just what she said."

I took the bag from him. Something about it was so familiar. As I held it in my hand, I remembered our trip to the mall, and Mom's bag with the hanger—*just a little something for myself,* she had said.

I pulled up the bag slowly, nervously. I saw a flash of blue, cornflower blue, the color of a cloudless summer day. The tears came on so quickly I didn't have time to stop them; they just rolled down my face.

Patrick moved in and put his arm around me. "It's okay, Missy," he said in a soothing voice, like Mom would to Claude. "It's going to be just fine. Who cares what you wear? You look great."

I had picked the awful dress to hurt Patrick, too. And now he was being so nice. Since everything that happened in the field we hadn't said much more than, "pass the toast" to one another. And now this?

"Patrick," I said, pulling away. "You haven't even said sorry."

"For what, Missy?"

"For lying to me. Betraying me."

"It's all about you, isn't it, Missy? Like Moose and Lyle—"

"Don't talk about Moose. I don't want to talk about them."

"Don't you want to know the whole story?"

"I know the whole story."

"Can you even try to see a situation from a side you're not standing on?"

"Nobody can."

"Sure they can. Like with Mom and Dad. You always blame Dad for their divorce, but Mom was part of it, too."

"She didn't leave us."

"Dad didn't leave us, Missy. He didn't even leave Mom. *They* split up. End of story."

"That's the easy way to see it, Patrick."

"Missy, that's how you are with Shauna. And Moose and Lyle, too. One person is always right and one is wrong. It's not like that. Life isn't always like that."

"Well, what you did was wrong."

"So what if it was? And what if Dad was wrong, too? Are you going to hate him for the rest of your life? Are you going to hate me?"

"Yes," I said. "I think so." But I couldn't stop the smile at the corner of my mouth. It felt so good to be talking to Patrick again. But then I remembered that I hated him. "So, did you kiss her?"

"What?"

"Do you guys kiss?"

"Yeah."

"What's it like?"

"I can't describe it. You'll find out for yourself, someday."

"I won't."

"You will."

"Why do you like her so much?"

"She likes me."

"A lot of people like you."

"It's different, Missy." Patrick was thoughtful for a moment, the way that Patrick gets when he's trying to decide if he wants to speak or not. Finally he got up and crossed to the other side of the room. He stood in front of my dresser mirror and didn't look at me when he spoke.

"I never told you this but something happened at the end of the school year. It was after gym and I was getting dressed. Some boys grabbed me and shoved me out of the locker room. Then they held the door so I couldn't get back in. They kept shouting, 'Come and see the amazing stick boy,' and pretty soon other kids came to see what all the yelling was about. And there I was."

"Naked?"

"No, I had on my underwear and socks."

Quickly I made a mental note: Always put pants and shirt directly over gym clothes. "Well," I said, softening in spite of myself. "Oh."

"The gym teacher came pretty quickly, but still, a few kids saw me and it was the big joke." Patrick's face had gone pale, just thinking about it.

"Well, I'm sorry." I said it grudgingly.

"It's okay. It's just one of those things that happen. Some of those guys, they were my friends even."

"I don't get it."

"That's just it. Sometimes you can't get people. You just can't. Like Mom and Dad. We can't totally get it. But we can get that they're both trying to be our mom and dad still."

"Dad's not," I said. "He's getting married to someone else today. And I will never forgive him."

"Then it will be your loss."

"You sound like them."

"I'm not them, Missy. I'm me. Patrick—your brother."

"So what about Shauna?"

"What about her?"

"What's so great about her?"

"Well, she's funny. And she's fun. We laugh together. And she's, you know—"

"Yeah, yeah. Miss Bikini Top."

Patrick ignored me. "That's why I told you about the thing in the gym. I've always felt embarrassed about how I look. But not with Shauna. When I'm around her, I don't feel like I need to hide my legs. Like at the lake. I just have fun. I feel like myself."

"What about your limp?"

"See, that's just it, Missy. I don't think I even limp that much anymore, but you still see me that way. You see me as your skinny brother who limps."

"Well, you do. One of your legs is shorter than the other. It's a fact."

"By a half a millimeter or something. The doctor measured. It's not as big a difference as it used to be. Do you even know what a millimeter is?"

"Sure," I said. But I didn't. And I wondered something about myself right then. Why did I still *want* Patrick to be a limper?

Patrick turned to look straight at me. "Anything else?" he asked.

What I wanted to say to him was this: *The best part of the summer had been walking down that tire-track road with you in the morning, side by side.* But I knew if I did, I would start to cry again. So instead I pointed to my Looks Can Kill outfit. "Do you think I should wear this?"

"It's up to you, Missy," Patrick said. "I'll stand by you no matter what."

CHAPTER 48

ACROSS THE HALL IN THE BATHROOM, I YANKED AND pulled and peeled myself out of the spandex war dress. Then I took the cornflower blue off the hanger and slipped it over my head. It fell around me like a soft breeze.

I stared at the mirror. The girl across from me looked nice. She looked good. She looked like me, only in a perfect dress.

I thought about my mother, back home, drinking tea out of the cup with our smiling younger faces. *"Thanks, Mom,"* I whispered, hoping that somehow she could hear me.

When I walked back to my room, Patrick was just as I'd left him, except his face was now flushed with something new, like excitement or nervousness or both. For the first time I noticed that the fancy suit hung too big around his bony shoulders.

"It's time, Missy," he said. "We should go down."

We were about to go downstairs to a backyard bursting with people and flowers. We were about to stand underneath a gazebo decorated with white ribbons and red roses while our father proclaimed his love and commitment to someone who was not our mother. What in life could I believe in? What could I trust?

"Patrick," I said, "the next time you lie to me, or abandon me, or do something that destroys—"

"Okay, Missy," he said.

"Okay what?"

"I won't. Ever again. Can we please just drop it?"

I tried to get him to look me in the eye. I glared hard. He barely met my gaze, but I could tell it wasn't out of shame or guilt or anything like that. His thoughts were completely with what was about to happen instead of what had already happened. Maybe they were with Shauna, even. He was moving away. That's what people did.

And me? What about me?

I sat down on the bed, cornflower blue falling around me like a perfect summer sky. I thought about Moose and Lyle, their father and the Little Field and what Al had told me about the blood feud. I thought about Bev's ghost boys, reminding her of happier days. How easy it would be to let one another slip past and not let any of it matter.

Everyone needs to find a way to make peace with the humanity of others, Al had said to me that day. *That just might be your bigger lesson out here.*

Was that what it had all been about? A lesson? And if I couldn't learn it, then would everything that happened ever add up to anything more than some bills stuffed in a jar underneath my bed?

Patrick held out his arm. "We should go," he said.

Could it be that simple? Could I just stand up and take his arm and forget all that happened? Walk down to our father's wedding smiling like I meant it?

"You go ahead," I said. "I'll be down in a minute."

"Come on, Missy," he said, and held out his arm again.

"I said go ahead!" I was afraid that if I breathed I would cry, so I held my breath.

"Missy." Patrick dropped his arm and looked straight into my eyes. And then he said it—the one thing I needed, the only thing that would work. "I can't do this without you," he said. "I just can't."

My brother. My Patrick.

I nodded until I could finally speak. "Okay," I said at

last. I stood and straightened my dress. "Okay."

"Hey, I just remembered something else." Patrick reached into his jacket pocket. I saw a flash of white. "Your friends told me to give this to you."

"What?"

"Constance and Allie. I saw them at the lake. You wouldn't call them back, so they told me to give this to you on Dad's wedding day. They said to look for them."

I reached out and took the brand-new pair of 3-D glasses from his hand. The lenses had been removed and the front was perfectly decorated with shiny white fabric and my favorite color glitter glue. It even had a new Spectacular Button, tiny and red.

"Here?" I said. "They won't be here. Not after how I acted—"

"Of course they're here, Missy."

Heart pounding, I ran across the hall to Patrick's room, where the big window overlooked the backyard. I saw Claude, happy in the arms of one of the Cleveland people. And then, there they were, standing against the back fence, wearing pretty dresses and, yes, 3-D glasses!

"Missy?" Patrick said from the doorway.

Putting on my own glasses, I spun back around. And maybe it was because I'd moved so fast, or the room was too hot, or my Spectacular Button was pushed to high, or

I'd just been thinking about Moose and Lyle, or my eyes were filled with tears. I don't know. But that's when I saw them, just a flash of them. I saw our younger selves, Patrick and me, our own paper-thin ghost selves. They surrounded us. They played and fought and danced at our feet.

"Patrick! Did you just see that?"

"What?"

They had lasted as long as a blink, just long enough to let me know they were there, that maybe they would always be there. Because, really, where else could they go? Who else would know to take care of them?

"What is it, Missy?"

I shook my head. I closed my eyes and opened them again. "Nothing. I guess I was just remembering. That's all. I was just remembering when we were little."

"We should get down there." Patrick took a deep, nervous breath and, once again, held his arm out to me. "You look good, Missy."

I looked at him gratefully. "You too."

"Really?" He tugged at his sagging pants. "Does this suit look too big on me?"

"No," I said, seeing my brother clearly, in Spectacular 3-D. "You look perfect. You look just right."

I took off my glasses and left them there on the

windowsill, overlooking the gazebo and the flowers and the new step-relatives from Ohio and my very best friends.

Then I took Patrick's arm and held on tight. And together we walked out the door, across the hall, and down the stairs. To our father's wedding.

ONE LAST THING

A WEEK AFTER THE NEW SCHOOL YEAR STARTED, A package arrived for me in the mail, with a letter attached. The package was about the size of a shoebox. I read the letter before opening the package.

Dear Melissa,

Al said that you came by to see us. Both myself and Bev are sorry we missed you. You were the best picker we had and we hope you will come back next year to pick for us again.

    The Little Field is doing just fine. Those kids didn't hurt the bushes at all, just took the

berries. I don't mind so much. Al told me what
you said about feeling it was your fault and I
appreciate the sentiment but want you to know
that sometimes things just happen. I don't
believe for one minute it is your fault. Not one
minute.

There is one other thing. I don't know if you
recall, but in the Little Nickel advertisement
there was an announcement about a prize to the
best picker. Well by my calculations that would
be you. So here is your prize. Wear it proud and
know that we farmers need to stick together.

Warmest regards,

Moose

Carefully, I opened the box, unwrapped the tissue,
and lifted out my prize. It was a brand-new, bright green
hat with a yellow stag, just like the one I saw Moose wear
out in the field, every day. And it took me right back,
to dewy cold mornings and sticky hot afternoons. To
wildflowers and honeybees and old trucks and tire-track
roads. Clanging buckets and old-man stories and tangy
Kool-Aid and award-winning cherry pie. It made me
think of Moose, who loved his plants like they were his

family. And even after all that happened, he still trusted me with his family. The bright green hat took me there, to all of that. So I put it on. And I wrote a letter back.

> *Dear Moose and Bev,*
>
> *Thank you for the hat. It fits perfectly. I will wear it next summer, when I am working in the fields again. I can't wait.*

I signed it,

> *Your friend, Missy.*

ACKNOWLEDGMENTS

Thanks to my trusty group of early readers: Heather Barbieri, Trilby Cohen, Sarah Conradt, Danika Dinsmore, Michael Hagan, George Laney, Colleen Preston, Simon Schwartz. Extra-credit thanks to Matthew Reid-Schwartz, who read every single word of every single draft. And Sarah, also, for the blueberry bushes. And Alex Kuo and Joan Burbick, always.

Thanks to SCBWI for helping me put all my pieces together.

Thanks to my agent, Liza Pulitzer Voges, for her upbeat ways and unflappable encouragement.

Thanks to Melissa Faulner, Rosanne Lauer, Irene Vandervoort, and everyone at Penguin Random House who worked to support this book and make it shine.

So many thanks to my editor, Julie Strauss-Gabel, who asked the right questions and then continued to ask (patiently, thoughtfully) until I got to the heart of each answer. The best parts of this story came from those questions. Really.

Thanks to my parents, Sue and C.J. Nickerson, who let summers be about digging holes, learning to grow things, and playing outside, way past dark. Thanks also to my brothers, Dan, Dave, Jay, and Jim, who remember the details, fill in my blanks, and are some of the best storytellers I know.

Thanks to my sons, Simon and Jasper, for their good humor and perspective.

And thanks beyond thanks to my husband, Matthew. For his inspiration, patience, smarts, musical accompaniment, and everything else.